# POLLY

## Marion Chesney
### writing as Jennie Tremaine

G.K.HALL &CO.
Boston, Massachusetts
1987

Published in Large Print by arrangement
with Dell Publishing Co., Inc.

G. K. Hall Large Print Book Series.

Set in 16pt Plantin.

**Library of Congress Cataloging in Publication Data**

Chesney, Marion.
   Polly.

   (Nightingale series) (G. K. Hall large print book
series)
   1. Large type books.   I. Title.
[PR6053.H4535P57   1987]      823'.914      87–8807
ISBN 0–8161–4356–0 (lg. print)

For Sharon and David Chesney

# POLLY

# CHAPTER ONE

One more household chore to do and then she would have the rest of Sunday to prepare for her first job. And she had the house to herself.

Polly Marsh poured cold water onto the cake of black lead that stood in a jam jar by the kitchen sink and absentmindedly began mixing it into a paste. Every Sunday it was her job to blacklead the kitchen range until it shone. The range was the center of the Marsh household. It took up a complete wall of the little kitchen. There was the boiler on one side and the oven on the other. In the middle was the fire, with an iron bar across the top for hanging the kettle or the frying pan.

The range took an hour to polish and then the steel fender had to be scrubbed with emery paper and then buffed to a high shine.

Polly automatically went about her work, half listening to the cries and shouts of the traders in the street below. Stone Lane Market in London's Shoreditch was in full Sunday swing.

1

The other members of the Marsh household, Polly's mother and father, grandmother, and little brother and sister were all downstairs in the shop selling fruit and vegetables as hard as they could.

Marshes had been greengrocers in Stone Lane for as long as anyone could remember. Every morning, Polly's father, Alf, would rise with the sun and push his wooden barrow to Covent Garden Market to get the best prices. It was hard work, but the Marsh family had been able to buy the two flats above the shop and convert them into one household. Polly had that unheard-of luxury in Shoreditch—a room of her own. And the Marsh family had one other luxury that was the envy of the neighborhood: The kitchen in the top flat had been converted into a bathroom with *running water*. The neighbors had shaken their heads and prophesied everything from pneumonia to tuberculosis as a result of this unheard-of cleanliness. But they envied them just the same. Hot baths suggested a world of luxury far removed from noisy, working-class Shoreditch.

Still dreaming, Polly gave the range a final polish and lit the fire. Tomorrow morning she would leave Stone Lane and walk across all those mysterious class boundaries to start work in the City of London. Not only in the City but in a company owned by a real-live duke.

Westerman's was the name of the import-export firm that had graciously agreed to employ Miss Polly Marsh as a stenographer.

Polly could still remember the pale March sunlight sparkling on the ducal coat of arms over the door, the quiet musty interior, and the dreaded interview. She had acquitted herself well and had been inordinately pleased when Mr. Baines, the manager, had asked her if she was a foreigner, as her voice was completely without accent. Polly had smiled and shaken her head and sent up a prayer of thanks for her elocution lessons.

The elocution lessons had been the brainchild of her schoolteacher, Miss James. Miss James had assured Polly's mother that a girl with startlingly good looks and superior intelligence should not be condemned to go through life with a hideous cockney accent. She had recommended a retired elocution teacher, who would give lessons for a small sum. In a more middle-class environment, Polly's

3

newly refined voice would have caused acid comment, but the cockneys of the market were proud of anyone who wanted to get on and simply called Polly 'the duchess,' with their usual nonchalant friendly good humor.

Polly glanced in the oval mirror on the wall and shuddered. She seemed to be black from head to foot. That was the curse of black lead. No matter how careful you were, the stuff seemed to creep out of the cleaning rag and end up all over your body.

She scrubbed herself down vigorously in the bathroom upstairs and then began to carefully make her preparations for her working debut. First her hair had to be shampooed. She shaved a precious bar of Knight's Castille soap into a cup and mixed it into a paste with hot water, then added a teaspoon of alcohol to remove any excess oil from her hair. Next, she added a teaspoon of cologne to perfume it. A large jug of chamomile tea stood ready for the final rinse.

Next came the manicure—the cuticles to be pushed back with an orange stick with a small piece of cotton on the tip dipped in cuticle acid and then the stick run under the tips of the nails in order to remove any stains. The nails had to be cut into an oval shape and smoothed with the emery board. And then Polly came to the final step in her manicure—the application of her precious hoard of nail polish. She carefully dipped the buffer into the powder and drew it back and forth across her nails, with light, even strokes, until they gleamed and shone.

With the daring purchase of nail polish, she had also bought rose-tinted rice powder—so much more expensive than the ordinary kind, which had a cheap metallic base—and real bone hairpins, instead of wire ones. She had toyed with the idea of buying a lipstick but a beauty article in *Queen* magazine had said that this cosmetic could thicken the skin of the lips, and who on earth wanted that to happen?

Now all she had to do was stitch sweat pads into her new serge business dress and brush up her best felt hat, polish her button boots, and leave her corset by the window to air. Thank goodness it wasn't raining, otherwise the newly cleaned corset would have had to be hung up on the pulley in the kitchen and by now would be smelling of Ma's roast beef and bubble and squeak.

These last chores completed, Polly sat down and gazed at herself in the mirror.

Her damp hair was already springing back into its familiar golden curls. She had a broad forehead and well-spaced wide blue eyes, a straight little nose, and a perfect mouth. *Beautiful*, thought Polly, not for the first time. *Absolutely beautiful.*

She had once thought that perhaps she had been adopted. For how could the bent little Alf Marsh and the cottage loaf Mary Marsh have produced such a beauty? But Mary Marsh had only grinned and shown Polly a photograph of herself, Mary, as a young girl. She had looked exactly like Polly and Polly had pouted for days. Gone were her secret dreams of being the cast-off daughter of an aristocrat!

Her mother's voice broke into her thoughts. 'Come along, Pol. We 'as fish-and-chips from Bernie's, as 'ot as 'ot. But if you sits up there much longer, luv, they'll be bleedin' cold!'

The Duchess of Stone Lane gave a disdainful sniff, but the thought of Bernie's fish-and-chips with perhaps a big pickled onion or two was too much for her. She ran down happily to join the rest of her family, who were already gathered around the kitchen table.

Gran was inhaling her tea with noisy

relish, baby Alf, a chubby five-year-old, was pleating the fringes of Gran's shawl, and nine-year-old Joyce was trying to eat fish-and-chips and read a comic at the same time.

Mrs. Marsh eased off her shoes and gave a groan of pleasure. 'Sit down, ducks,' she said as Polly came in. 'That's a luvly bit o' fish. Yerse. Tell you what, Pol, I was a-talking to Lil—you know, 'er what 'as the junk store—'bout Westerman's. Well, she says as 'ow the duke 'as got two sons and none of 'em is married.' Her small blue eyes twinkled wickedly at Polly from behind pads of fat. 'Think you'll marry one of 'em?'

Polly blushed with irritation. She *had* been thinking just that. She tossed her curls. 'They're probably too old.'

'Not a bit of it,' said Mrs. Marsh. 'Lil says that the elder is Edward, Marquis of Wollerton, and 'e 'as bin disappointed in love when 'e was a lad. 'E's thirty-six now. Yerse. And the young 'un is Lord Peter Burley and 'e's only twenty.'

Polly licked her fingers. 'How did Lil find out all this?'

''Er reads them society columns,' said Mrs. Marsh. 'Bring me my slippers, Joyce,

7

there's a luv.'

'Oh, *Ma*, I'd just got to the interesting bit,' wailed Joyce, clutching hold of her comic.

'Do as yer ma says or I'll tear off yer arm and hit yer with the soggy end,' snarled her father. Alf Marsh was, in fact, a timid, gentle man but he had a habit of uttering really terrible threats that fortunately no one, and least of all his children, took seriously.

'When I was 'er age . . .' began Gran, and Polly drifted off into dreamland.

Life had always seemed sunny and easy. She had passed her exams at school with hardly any study and she had learned shorthand and typing in under six months. The road to the future stretched out in her mind, broad and sunny, all the way to the altar with one of the duke's sons. Which one? The marquis sounded a bit old. But Lord Burley! Now he was only a year older than herself.

The remains of the fish-and-chips congealed in the newspaper as Polly pictured her first day at work.

'*Oh, Lord Peter! How you startled me!*' she would cry out when she turned to find him standing behind her.

'*Forgive me*,' he would mutter hoarsely. '*I am enchanted by your beauty . . .*'

'Wake up, Pol,' said her mother. 'Yer ladyship 'as still got some cleaning up to do!'

*I will, of course, hire her a maid*, thought Polly as she cleared away the tea things with a faint condescending smile. Meanwhile, she must suffer, like the best of Cinderellas.

Tomorrow would be a whole new life . . .

## CHAPTER TWO

The clocks of the City were chiming eight on a windy March Monday morning as Polly, clutching her hat, arrived at the worn front steps of Westerman's offices. The walk had taken longer than she expected, since various dreams of marrying into the aristocracy had slowed her steps.

Once into the narrow winding streets of the City, London's commercial hub, she had found herself wedged in a moving mass of men in tall silk hats and frock coats, all walking at a tremendous pace. Businesswomen were still a rarity in this masculine territory, and more than one paused his hurrying steps to stare appreciatively at the golden girl with the wide blue eyes and pink cheeks. Polly took it as her due. She was used to being stared at.

Mr. Baines was already there, fastening cardboard protectors on his wrist bands, as Polly blew into the dingy offices on a gale of March wind that sent the papers flying.

The heavy glass door crashed behind her and the dim, religious silence, which can only be created by a group of people slaving to the gods of wealth and industry, surrounded her.

Mr. Baines looked at the clock with some irritation. One minute past eight. This was what came from employing females, but stenographers were 'modern' and 'up-to-date' and Mr. Baines was human enough to share the up-to-date craze that was sweeping London.

'Take off your coat, Miss . . . ah . . . and I will begin dictating letters immediately.'

Polly removed her coat with nervous fingers. Four clerks were already seated on their high stools, bent over their ledgers. One of them caught Polly's eye and winked. She flushed and looked away. Cheek!

Mr. Baines was a small, slim, middle-aged man with a high celluloid collar and patent-leather hair. He had the small, twinkling humorous eyes of people who have usually no sense of humor.

'Now, Miss . . . ah . . . if you will follow me.' He led the way out of the outer office and along a long dark corridor, finally pushing open a door at the end.

'This will be your office, Miss . . . ah . . . I think it highly unsuitable that a young girl should have an office of her own but, on the other hand, it would be extremely unsuitable if you were to work with the men.'

Polly stared around her in dismay. The 'office' was little more than a dingy cubicle with a small, chipped and battered wooden table on which stood a black and gleaming typewriter decorated with feminine scrollwork. The typewriter had been considered a female instrument from the day it was first invented and the manufacturers still made considerable efforts at gentility by decorating their machines with gilt-stenciled decoration.

There was a peg to hang her coat, a wooden filing cabinet, a pile of dusty ledgers from which protruded scraps of yellowing paper showing that the room had been previously used as a dump, a small gas fire, and wood-paneled walls, dark with age.

Polly did not know that Mr. Baines was as nervous as herself. It was a big day for him. Instead of scribbling his business letters and then handing them over to a clerk to make a fair copy, he would be able to sit and dictate. *Very* up-to-date. He had not yet told his business friends whom he met daily at lunchtime in the chop house around the corner about it. But he fancied he might just drop a little word today.

Especially to Bloggs.

Bloggs with his beery face and large mustache would shout as usual, 'Here comes our relic of the Dark Ages. What you been doing this morning, Baines? Sharpening up the quill pens?'

And in his mind's eye Mr. Baines could see himself casually raising his tankard and taking a slow pull before remarking carelessly, 'Oh, nothing special, old boy. Spent the whole morning dictating letters to my secretary.'

And wouldn't Bloggs stare!

Not that he meant to tell Polly that she ranked as a secretary. That sort of thing gave girls ideas above their station.

Polly opened her bag and produced a large notebook and sat down primly behind the desk, while Mr. Baines prowled up and down. He cleared his throat. He said, 'To Messrs. Thistlewood and Jamieson, 22 Victoria Street, Singapore. Dear Sirs . . .'

The working day had begun.

Mr. Baines dictated letter after letter, while Polly made a mental note to study her school atlas when she got home that evening. All the addresses seemed to be in the farthest-flung parts of the British Empire.

Mr. Baines droned on, the gas fire hissed and popped, and Polly began to think that lunchtime would never come. She had an overwhelming desire to go to the lavatory and did not know if she could last another minute.

She firmly crossed her legs under the desk and tried to concentrate as her face got redder and redder. There was nothing for it. Social conventions must be thrown to the wind. Mr. Baines had finished one letter and was about to start another when Polly spoke up. Her voice sounded to her ears as if it was coming from very far away.

'I beg to be excused, Mr. Baines.'

'Why?'

'I would like to leave the room, sir,' said Polly, feeling as if she were back at school.

Mr. Baines looked at her with dawning comprehension. Now it was his turn to blush. 'Well, really Miss ... ah ... I'm afraid that is something that has been overlooked. Can you not contain yourself until lunchtime? There is a ... er ... place for ladies opposite the Bank.'

Polly shook her head firmly.

'Oh, dear, dear. Follow me,' he said, leading her back along the winding corridors and down a flight of twisty wooden steps to the basement. Mr. Baines lit a candle with maddening slowness. 'No gas laid on here I'm afraid. There is the ... er ... yes, behind that door.'

Polly was in too much agony to be embarrassed. She dived into the lavatory, which was fortunately lit by a small barred window, since Mr. Baines had kept the candle.

She emerged a few minutes later to find a much-shaken Mr. Baines standing guard outside.

'I shall leave you to type those letters, Miss ... ah ... and in future, you will need to make your own arrangements. It

14

would be very distressing if any of the gentlemen should find you here. You really must consider their feelings, Miss ... ah ...'

He extinguished the candle and fled up the stairs, leaving Polly to find her own way back to her room. She stared around in bewilderment and then slowly moved along the corridor. Was this it? Six men with bristling mustaches, looking for all the world like a meeting of walruses, were seated around a large mahogany table. They all stared at her with outraged expressions on their faces as she hurriedly closed the door. She turned around and nearly bumped into the cheeky clerk who had winked at her. But she needed help. 'I'm lost,' she said. 'Can you show me to my office?'

'Certainly,' said the young man. 'I will even slay dragons for you. My name is Bob Friend, as in friendly. I am your servant. I fall at your feet.'

'Simply show me to my office, Mr. Friend, I have work to do,' replied Polly in chilly accents.

'Of course,' he answered with a grin. 'This way, my lady. Will my lady be partaking of lunch? I would be glad to offer my humble escort.'

Polly opened her mouth to refuse. But the thought of venturing out into the masculine City on her own was frightening. She would never find out anything about the mysterious duke and his sons, locked away in her cubicle, either. And Mr. Friend was quite pleasant-looking, with a plump, cherubic face and an unruly mop of brown curls.

She forced herself to smile at him. 'I should be glad of someone to show me to a place to eat.'

'Good!' said Mr. Friend. 'I'll call at your palace in half an hour.' He pushed open the door to Polly's office, gave her a cheery wave, and bustled off down the corridor. Polly mentally resolved to draw a map or make chalk marks on the wall on the way out so that she should not lose her way again. Why, those terrifying men with the walrus mustaches could be complaining about her to Mr. Baines right at this minute!

She had typed half of the letters, neatly and rapidly, by the time Mr. Friend popped his curly head around the door.

Mr. Friend had decided to brave Spielmann's, the chophouse where Mr.

16

Baines usually ate. It was more than he could afford and he felt sure Mr. Baines would be furious to see him there, but one lunch with this gorgeous girl was surely worth eating saveloys from the street vendor for the rest of the week.

Mr. Baines was just savoring his triumph over Mr. Bloggs when Bob and Polly pushed their way through the crowd at the bar to find a table in the small room beyond. The crowd of men fell silent and all heads turned. To see a woman in Spielmann's was rare enough, but to see such a beauty!

Crimson with pride, Bob found a corner table and drew Polly's chair out for her.

'Well, bless my soul!' cried Mr. Baines. 'That's my secretary with one of my clerks!'

Mr. Bloggs wiped the foam from his mustache and stared at Mr. Baines in open admiration. 'Why, Baines,' he said slowly, 'you *old dog*.'

Mr. Baines drank his beer in a rosy glow. Never had anyone looked at him in admiration before. He stood primly and quietly as usual, but inside, his ink-stained soul swaggered with all the bravado of the veriest masher.

'Now, what would you like, Miss . . .

ah . . .' Bob Friend was saying.

'Oh, I'm tired of being called Miss Ah,' said Polly, picking up her soup-stained menus. 'My name is Miss Marsh.' She looked at the menu. There was businessman's lunch special for one shilling and sixpence but it still seemed like an awful lot of money, especially as Mr. Friend would have to pay for her lunch.

Polly was vain, but she had a great deal of her mother's maternal good nature in her character. 'I suggest, Mister Friend,' she said in her clear, light voice, 'that if I pay for my own, we could possibly afford another lunch together. I certainly cannot afford these prices every day and neither, I suppose, can you.'

'Don't spoil my big moment,' pleaded Bob. 'All the fellows in the room are envying me like mad.'

'It's all right, *really*,' said Polly. 'I'll slip you the money at the end of the meal and nobody will be any the wiser.' She looked at him with her large blue eyes and Mr. Friend felt as if he were deliciously drowning in a tropical sea.

'Furthermore,' Polly went on, 'if you don't let me pay, I shall not have lunch with you again.'

'Oh, in that case,' said the much dazzled Bob, 'I will—I mean, you can pay.'

The businessman's special turned out to be very good value. They had Scotch broth followed by mutton chops, and rounded it off with large slabs of treacle tart and custard.

Demolishing it all with a healthy appetite, Polly still managed to find time to pick Mr. Friend's brain. 'How many staff has Westerman's?'

'Hard to say,' said Bob. 'I have only been working several months in the labyrinth. But there are the company directors with their various offices and secretaries—men, of course—then all the people who deal with the goods that pour in and out of the warehouses down on the Thames, as well as Mr. Baines, the clerks, such as myself, the office boys, the messengers, the accountants, the bookkeepers, and ... oh ... one other female.'

Polly stiffened. She was just beginning to enjoy being alone in this man's world. The female was a Miss Amy Feathers who operated the small switchboard, but one hardly ever saw her.

'What is she like?' said Polly.

'Well, small and ... well, all right,' said

Bob Friend, callously forgetting that until this glorious morning, he had found Miss Feathers quite attractive.

With all the aplomb of a true businessman Polly waited until the last crumb of treacle tart was gone before she presented her all-important question.

Resting her small chin on her hands, she leaned forward and inquired as casually as she could, 'The Duke of Westerman, now. Is it quite a thrill when he comes to the office?'

'Oh, he doesn't,' said Bob Friend cheerfully, unaware that he was plunging a dagger of disappointment right through the new serge dress and into Polly's heart. 'Westerman's was started by some younger son ... oh, about fifty years ago. Great scandal it was ... one of them sort going into trade. He traveled all over the Orient, setting up deals and buying up merchandise—made millions by the time he was thirty, so they say. Meanwhile, *that* Duke of Westerman and his family were going broke. So this younger son takes to smoking opium, but by that time Westerman's had its board of directors and was running very well.

'Well, now comes the big scandal. *This*

here duke, he inherits the title back in the 1880s and it looks as if the family estate is going to have to go up for sale. But the younger son, he dies in a den in Limehouse and the Westermans all turn up their long noses and say "that's what comes of going into trade." 'Course, they soon sing a different song when they find he's left them the firm and all the millions. So they live in luxury and don't trouble their heads about the firm. The directors know their jobs and Baines is a good manager. Why should they?'

'Why should they, indeed,' echoed Polly in a hollow voice. 'And the duke's sons?'

'Them neither,' said Bob. 'The young 'un's at Oxford and a bit of a rip, by all accounts, and the elder, the marquis, he runs the estates. Mad keen on aggericultoor and hunting and fishing and all that. Them's not going to come near the office.'

The crowded chophouse had seemed a warm, romantic place, with its shining oak and brass rails and warm smells of food and beer, only a moment before. Now, to Polly, it seemed nothing more than a dingy, greasy tavern.

She had entered like a princess. Now, she left, very much like Miss Polly Marsh,

21

stenographer—wages, ten shillings a week.

The March wind whipped along the City streets, carrying on its wings a faint balmy suggestion of daffodils on lawns and crocuses in hedgerows, and pale-yellow sunlight gilded the dome of St. Paul's and glistened on the bobbing sea of tall hats as the City returned to its afternoon's work. Polly plunged into the gloom of the office, feeling as if she had left the whole of the world behind.

She finished the rest of the letters quickly and took them in to Mr. Baines to sign. The fact that he seemed startled at her speed and accuracy and that he actually smiled at her did nothing to lift the gloom from Polly's heart. How on earth was she ever going to find her rightful niche in society now?

Mr. Baines gave her an enormous pile of invoicing as if to prove that no matter how quick she was, work at Westerman's was never done. As she turned around to leave, he called her back into his large, musty office, which was off the clerks' room.

'Oh, Miss ... ah ... I have already informed some of the staff of the honor that has been conferred on us. His Grace, the Duke of Westerman, has suggested that the annual staff picnic—that is usually held on the first of June—take place on the grounds of his ancestral home, Bevington Chase. Us gentlemen of the staff are allowed to bring our wives. The bachelors, like Mister Friend, can bring a lady of their choice. No mention, however, has been made of any lady in the firm bringing a gentleman. . .'

'Oh, *that's* all right, Mister Baines,' said Polly, her eyes shining like stars.

'Very well, Miss . . . ah . . . you may go.'

Polly's feet barely seemed to touch the floor on her way back to her cubicle.

It was nearly the end of March—two whole months to go. She found she had neatly typed, 'To one consignment of Dukes,' and tore up the invoice and concentrated on her work. It would never do to lose her job before the picnic.

Back in Stone Lane that evening Polly's great news was received with infuriating calm. 'I'm trying to finish this story,' said Joyce, clutching a tattered edition of *Young England*. 'This 'ere cavaleer is trying for to get away from them roun'eads. Leave me alone, Pol.'

'Sit yourself down, luv,' said Mrs. Marsh. 'I've got some nice pigs' trotters saved for you. I'll 'ear all about your dukes when you've eaten.'

Polly sighed. Would her family never appreciate the aristocrat in their midst? But Mrs. Marsh was waiting with her plump red arms folded until Polly finished the last of her meal. 'The bread queues are getting wurst,' she said, shaking her frizzled hair. 'If some of them poor souls could see you, Pol, a-picking at your food. Well, I dunno wot they would say.'

'Yerse. Eat up,' admonished her father, 'or I'll tear yer 'ead off.'

'Now,' said Mrs. Marsh, sitting down beside Polly. 'Wot's it all about?'

Trembling with excitement, Polly told her about the picnic, the stately home, the invitation, and the date. 'Oh, Ma! Could I . . . could I have a tea gown to wear?'

Mrs. Marsh narrowed her small eyes thoughtfully. They had once been as large and as blue as Polly's but rosy pads of fat had diminished their size and hours of needlework had faded their color.

Perhaps in a more genteel working-class environment Polly's suggestion would have been greeted with horror. After all, she had two good dresses for winter and two for summer, not to mention the latest in long corsets. What girl could ask for more?

24

But among the traders of Stone Lane Market there was a good bit of the theater. When they emerged from their dark, cluttered shops on Sunday to sell their wares at the stalls outside, they competed for customers as hard as any circus barker. Everyone in Stone Lane knew that it was always possible to find what you wanted if you gave it a bit of time.

'Let me see,' said Mrs. Marsh. 'I've got it! Lil's stepsister, Edie, 'er wot 'as arthuritis, used to be a theater dresser. Went with the road production of *Lady Something-or-Other's Fanny.*'

'*Lady Windermere's Fan*,' corrected Polly faintly.

'Anyway,' pursued Mrs. Marsh, 'Edie kept some of them there costumes for sentimental reasons, like, yer see. I'll ask 'er termorrer if 'er still 'as that lacy thing from Act Two, she said it were.'

'But a *stage* costume!' protested Polly.

'Oh, it'll be same as the real thing. It waren't the Hippodrome yer know. Edie did luvly work afore her arthuritis got 'er.'

Gran surfaced from her cup of tea to say hoarsely, 'Don't you go dressin' above your station, Pol. They'll think you're a tart, that's wot.'

'No they won't,' snapped Polly. 'No one knows I come from . . .' Her voice faltered.

'No one knows yer comes from a dump like this,' her mother finished for her, with unimpaired good humor. 'But 'ave a care, my girl. Gran's right. Go careful.'

'Of course,' said Polly, practicing a haughty stare.

'What's 'appened to your face?' asked Joyce, looking over the top of *Young England*.

'It's them pigs' trotters,' said Alf Marsh. 'I've bin belchin' and fartin' like a locomotive.'

Polly rose from the table defeated. She would practice her haughty stare on young Mr. Friend in the morning.


## CHAPTER THREE

No matter how much Polly fretted, the months of April and May seemed to crawl along as they had never done before. The days grew longer and longer and the asthmatic old clock on the wall of Westerman's office hiccuped and coughed and wheezed, reluctantly surrendering each minute up as if to belie the TEMPUS FUGIT written on its yellow face.

At last the glorious day of the first of June arrived. It was a Saturday, of course, since frivolities such as staff outings were not allowed to take place during business hours.

Bevington Chase lay ten miles outside Chelmsford in Essex. The office party was to take a special train to Chelmsford and then proceed by charabanc to the duke's home. Polly had other travel plans. She meant to make a grand entrance. She had lied to Mr. Baines, telling him that she would be spending the night with an aunt in Chelmsford and that she would make her own way to the party.

Polly had then traveled to Chelmsford on the Saturday before the picnic to arrange the hire of a smart brougham and pair to drive her in style to Bevington Chase. It had taken all her savings but she felt it was well and truly worth it.

In her mind's eye Lord Peter would rush forward to assist her from the carriage, his eyes gleaming with admiration.

Saturday morning dawned sparkling and sunny. Polly carefully dressed herself in Lady Windermere's tea gown (Act Two). It was a beautiful thing made of cobweb-fine blond lace over a rose silk underdress and— miracle of miracles—Lil's stepsister, Edie, had produced a long pair of elbow-length pink kid gloves to go with it. Polly dressed her blond curls low on her brow in the current fashion and then placed an enormous hat of swathes of pink tulle on top. Her family had presented her with a pink lace parasol with an ivory handle, bought for surprisingly little money from Alf's second cousin, who was in the rag-and-bone business, and who had collected it from a dustbin up in the West End. It had obviously been thrown away because it wouldn't open, but a few delicate touches from old Solly, the clock repairer on the corner of Stone Lane, had made it as good as new.

Her pink kid reticule had been lent for the day by Mrs. Battersby in the tenement next door, who worked fourteen hours a day to make leather goods for the West End stores. And Bernie's fat, cheerful wife, Liz, who worked day and night behind the frier in the fish-and-chip shop, had lent a string of cultured pearls.

Feeling very strange and quite unlike herself, Polly descended the narrow stairs to the kitchen, where her family were assembled to see her on her way. 'Pwitty,' screamed little Alf, trying to grab her dress with jammy fingers and being seized in time by Joyce. Gran and Mrs. Marsh stared at her, their eyes filling with sentimental tears and even Alf Marsh cleared his throat. He was sweating in all the misery of his black Sunday suit and hard bowler hat, for he was to take Polly in a hansom to the railroad station.

'Come along, girl,' said Mr. Marsh, holding out his arm. 'Cor, it feels like I was father of the bride!'

They made their way downstairs and out into Stone Lane, where all the friends and neighbors had gathered. They sent up a resounding cheer as Polly appeared on the arm of her father. And Polly, who had meant to be very *grande dame* indeed, felt her eyes filling with grateful tears, and smiled and thanked them all instead.

Alf saw Polly into a third-class compartment when they arrived at the station. 'Don't speak to any mashers, now,' he cautioned. 'And 'ere, these are for you,' he added gruffly. He pulled a bag of bull's-eyes out of his pocket.

It was a strange present to give such a

well-dressed young lady but Polly remembered how, when she was a child, her father would always sneak up to her room when she was in disgrace and give her a bull's-eye—one of those gigantic sweets that lasted for hours and changed all colors of the rainbow when you sucked it.

She gave him a fierce hug. The whistle blew and Alf climbed out of the railway carriage.

'Keep the window closed,' he said, as the train began to steam out of the station, 'or you'll get soot all over that dress.' The train gathered speed and she clung onto her hat as his last words faintly reached her—'And don't damage that there dress o' Edie's or I'll cut yer 'eart out.'

Polly was alone in the compartment. She had taken a later train than the rest of the office party. She gave the leather strap a jerk and pulled the window up and then sat back on the worn seat, watching with dreamy eyes as the houses of London Town swept past to be replaced by green rolling fields.

The train puffed on, belching a great column of black smoke that rolled and writhed across the summer fields.

By the time Chelmsford was reached,

Polly of Stone Lane had been left somewhere along the line and that well-known debutante, Miss Polly Marsh, shook the dust of the third-class carriage from her French heels and moved along the platform to take her rightful place in society.

Soon she was seated in the open brougham with her pink parasol unfurled as the carriage clattered over the sun-dappled cobblestones of Chelmsford.

Shortly after, the carriage had left the old town and was traveling along a succession of long green lanes, their hedgerows so high that it was like plunging into cool green tunnels. The leaves still had the fragile, translucent green of spring. White bramble flowers starred the rough grass on the steep banks and the air was heavy with the smell of lime and lilac.

The carriage came to a stop before a square lodge house and the lodge keeper ran out to open the gates. Polly bowed her head in a stately manner and the gatekeeper touched his forelock. She settled back in the carriage with a sigh of pure pleasure.

The two glossy brown horses clopped up the long avenue of limes. An ornamental lake came into view with swans floating elegantly across its smooth surface. Then

31

the trees disappeared and the driveway came to a fork. One road led to a huge mansion. Polly blinked. It was like a palace.

The once elegant Palladian mansion had grown considerably since the Westermans had taken over the younger son's riches and added on service wings, bachelor wings, vestibules, and porte cocheres with careless abandon.

The other road led to a white-and-red-striped marquee with tables spread out on the lawns. The whole of Westerman's was already gathered and Polly's sharp eyes could see no sign of any ducal personage, young or old.

A footman in claret-and-silver livery stood at the fork of the road. His task was to make sure that the members of the office party went toward the marquee and that the duchess's guests went to the house. His practiced eye took in the glossy brougham and the fashionable young lady. 'Straight ahead to the house,' he said.

The driver cracked his whip and the horses clopped forward toward the imposing porticoed entrance.

Polly could feel her heart thudding against her stays. She knew somehow that she should have taken the other road to the marquee. But, then, was it her fault that she had been directed to the house?

A magisterial butler in a striped waistcoat opened the door and led her across a vast black-and-white-tiled entrance hall. He held aside a peach-colored portiere and opened a heavy mahogany door. 'Name, miss?'

'Miss Polly Marsh,' said Polly, feeling as if she had just burned her boats behind her.

'Miss Polly Marsh,' announced the butler in awesome tones.

Mary, Duchess of Westerman, rose to her feet, hoping that she did not look as puzzled as she felt. She had no recollection of having asked any Miss Polly Marsh, but then she *had* gone and got slightly squiffy at the Cartwrights' breakfast the other day and God only knew what she had said or whom she had invited.

She sailed forward with her usual aplomb. 'My *dear* Miss Marsh. We thought you were never going to get here. But now you *are* here, you're still in time for tea. You know everyone, don't you?' She realized her other guests were looking slightly bewildered. 'No? Then let me introduce you. Miss Tracy Otis from New

33

York, or do we say *Noo Yawk*—such a *quaint* accent—so *piquant*. Colonial people are such a *joy*. Just my little joke, Miss Otis.' Miss Otis, a pretty brunette, had had just about enough of happy English jests about colonials but she smiled frigidly and inclined her head. 'And let me see, Daisy Jennington and Mrs. Farthington-Bell and dear, dear Bubbles.' Bubbles was an elderly dowager who raised her lorgnette and surveyed Polly from head to foot. Polly could not imagine anyone less than a duchess daring to call her 'Bubbles.'

Polly sat down and was handed a fragile teacup and saucer. There was a little silence and then the other ladies began to talk. Polly refused the cake stand and then looked around the room. It seemed to be the beginning of a long succession of rooms stretching out into infinity. This one was crowded with photographs in silver frames. They were crammed onto every available space from the top of the piano to the fragile whatnots in the corners.

There was a portrait over the fireplace of a high-nosed lady in Regency dress who was wearing a purple turban. Her protruding blue eyes stared straight at Polly with cold hauteur.

Polly glanced up at the high painted ceiling. Various gods and goddesses were disporting themselves with the eighteenth century's interpretation of Greek abandon. A man with horns and goat's feet had one brown and muscular hand firmly clasped around the enormous breast of a simpering female. Polly felt her cheeks grow hot and wished she could find the courage to announce that she was in the wrong place and belonged with the office party. She eyed the duchess covertly and her heart sank.

The duchess was a formidable-looking lady with a great heavy head and a great heavy figure, which was draped in a sulphur-yellow tea gown. Her shoulders were covered with a dirty lace shawl and several of the sticks of her tortoiseshell fan were broken.

Bubbles, the dowager, again brought her lorgnette into play and transfixed Polly with two hideously enlarged eyes.

'Don't know any Marshes,' she said suddenly, 'except the Sussex ones. That your lot?'

'No. Kent,' said poor Polly, improvising wildly.

The duchess narrowed her eyes. She *must*

35

have been very squiffy indeed to have asked this girl. She wished people would stop calling these afternoon affairs where one drank too dreadfully much, 'breakfasts.' Well, she had better be extra nice to her in case the mysterious Miss Marsh realized that her hostess had been ... well, had had a little too much to drink.

'Darling Miss Marsh,' she ventured. 'I do adore your gown. Du-*veen*. And how are the Cartwrights?'

Polly sighed to herself. In for a penny, in for a pound. She gave her pretty laugh. 'Oh, the same old Cartwrights.'

'What was the name of that terribly funny German singer they insisted on dragging along? Sounded like a sneeze ... Frutz ... or Nitz ... or something.'

'Nietzsche,' said Polly desperately.

'I say, what an intellectual conversation,' drawled a voice from the doorway, and a languid young man ambled in.

'Now Peter. What do you mean by interrupting my tea party? You're supposed to put in an appearance with your brother at that Westerman picnic.'

'Oh, I'll join the ink-stained wretches later,' he laughed. He looked straight at Polly. 'Will someone introduce me?'

36

'This is Miss Polly Marsh, a *great* friend of the Cartwrights.'

Lord Peter bent over Polly's hand. 'Charmed,' he said. 'I'm really most awfully charmed.'

He was a tall, slim young man with glossy black hair worn rather long. His skin was very white and his eyes under their heavy lids were a vivid emerald green.

Polly's heart sang with happiness. Nothing could go wrong on this splendid day. The door opened and the duke himself bustled in. Ah, well, she would charm him to . . .

'Sorry to be so long, m'dear,' he was saying to his wife. 'But some damned stenographer female is missing from the party and Baines is worried that something might have happened to her. She lives in some infernal place . . . I've got it written down somewhere . . . going to phone the local cop shop and get them to send a bobby round to her address and find out if she left home this morning. I'll just go to my study.'

Polly got to her feet. Miserable, frightened, and quaking, she faced the room. Visions of an officer of the law arriving at her home and then telephoning back to say she had left and even—who knows?—giving a description of Stone Lane flashed across her terrified mind.

'I am that stenographer, Your Grace,' she said firmly. 'The footman in the drive directed me to the house. As I am practically the *only* lady at Westerman's, I thought Her Grace was going to entertain me separately.'

'But you said you knew the Cartwrights!' snapped the duchess.

'Obviously not the same family,' said Polly faintly.

'I should think *not*,' said the duchess. 'Fetch Jenkins,' she called to some servant out in the hallway. The ladies stared at Polly in frigid disdain with the exception of the young American, Miss Otis, who gave her a flicker of a wink.

The footman of the driveway, Jenkins, came into the room.

'Tell me, Jenkins,' said the duchess awfully, 'how it comes about that this person was shown to my tea instead of to the Westerman party?'

'She came in a private carriage, Your Grace,' said Jenkins glaring at poor Polly. 'I says that the Westerman party is over there and . . .'

'You did *not*,' said Polly. 'You told me to go straight to the house.'

'Well, well, no harm done,' said the duke jovially. 'I must say that Miss Marsh looks every bit as fetching as one of our society beauties. Jenkins, run along and tell Mr. Baines that his stenographer has been found and, Peter, it's time you helped your brother at the party. Escort Miss Marsh to the marquee.'

'Delighted!' said Lord Peter. 'This way, Miss Marsh.'

Jenkins had unfortunately collared Mr. Baines before Polly's arrival and had given Mr. Baines and the listening audience of Mr. Friend, Miss Feathers from the switchboard, the three other clerks, and sundry message boys a venomous description of Miss Marsh's presumption.

'Oh dear! Oh dear!' sighed Mr. Baines. 'Now I shall have to dismiss her. And she is such a good worker. Why, she had halved the office work. What got into the girl?'

His wife, Gladys, a bad-tempered-looking matron in cerise velvet, gave a contemptuous sniff. She was fed up with hearing nothing but Miss Marsh this and Miss Marsh that. Why, the girl was no better than she should be. 'You'd best tell his lordship, the marquis,' she said importantly.

'But, my dear, he is over there with the directors. I can hardly—'

'It's an excuse to put yourself forward,' hissed his wife. 'Go *on*!' She gave him a little push so that he half tottered toward where the Marquis of Wollerton was standing.

One of the directors, a choleric man called Sir Edward Blenkinsop, who had lost his digestion and his temper in India at Westerman's Bengal branch, eyed the unfortunate Mr. Baines.

'Well, Baines, found your girl yet?'

'Yes,' said Mr. Baines, turning his new gray bowler around and around in his clammy hands. 'There was a misunderstanding and she went to the house by mistake and the duchess thought she was one of Her Grace's guests.'

'She must be quite an enterprising young lady to have fooled Mama,' said a husky pleasant voice. Mr. Baines looked nervously at the Marquis of Wollerton. A pair of light-gold eyes looked amusedly back. Then the marquis glanced from the empurpled face of Sir Edward to the green-faced distress of Mr. Baines and added, 'I am sure you will find there has been some misunderstanding. Is this girl good at her work?'

'Oh, y-yes, my lord,' bleated Mr. Baines. 'Extremely competent girl, and a very hard worker.'

'You'll have to dismiss her,' barked Sir Edward.

'Come now, Sir Edward,' said the marquis lightly. 'You are assuming the girl to be vulgar and pushing. She is probably some quiet little thing who was directed to the house by mistake and was too overawed to open her mouth. Is that not so, Mister Baines?'

'Yes, indeed,' said Mr. Baines gratefully. Without his beautiful secretary he felt that he would return to being a mere nobody in the eyes of Bloggs & Co. He looked over the marquis's shoulder. 'Here comes Miss Marsh now.'

The marquis swung around and caught his breath. Escorted by his brother, Peter, Miss Polly Marsh floated across the smooth green lawn toward him. An errant breeze sent the blond cobweb lace of her tea gown swirling around her beautiful body, Danae in a shower of gold. Lord Peter carried his silk hat in his hand and his head was bent toward Polly's. They made a handsome couple—the epitome of young England on a summer's day.

The band of the Grenadier Guards had started to play selections from Gilbert and Sullivan on an improvised stand beside the marquee. Servants from the Chase bustled about laying out tea. All the smells of an English summer reached the marquis—hot tea, melting sugar, strawberries, methylated spirits from the stoves, roses, and freshly mown grass.

He was almost reluctant to hear Polly speak. An ugly voice would ruin such a pretty picture.

'Hullo, Peter, my boy. I see you've found the missing stenographer.'

'Oh, it was a riot,' said Peter boyishly. 'There was Mama, all social bristles like a porcupine. A *stenographer* at one of her teas!'

Polly flushed delicately and studied the ivory tip of her parasol.

She raised her eyes fleetingly to the marquis's face and then dropped them again. He did not look at all like his brother. In fact he looked quite terrifying. More people than Polly had found the marquis's looks awesome.

He had eyes of a peculiar light gold and heavy drooping eyelids. His nose was thin and high-bridged and his mouth long, thin, and mobile. His heavy brown hair was streaked with gold. He was well over six feet and carried himself with a languid hauteur that belied his muscular athletic body.

The more mischievous of his friends gleefully pointed him out to visiting Americans as 'the perfect British aristocrat.' The Americans were quite delighted with him as, before they had set eyes on the splendid marquis, they had been terribly disappointed to meet dukes who looked like plumbers and plumbers who looked like dukes.

'Miss ... ah ...' began Mr. Baines severely. 'Have the goodness to go and join the other members of the staff. I will have a word with you later. How came you to make such a mistake?'

'I'm very sorry, Mister Baines,' said Polly miserably. 'But I was directed to the house and I thought that, as I was about the only female in Westerman's, I was being ... er ... segregated.'

All the men, except Sir Edward, gave indulgent laughs but Mr. Baines had been

43

joined by his wife, Gladys, whose small eyes darted jealously over Lady Windermere's tea gown.

'You should be taught a lesson, my girl,' she said bitterly. 'Aping your betters, that's what. And I'd like to know where you got the money for that frock.'

Now, somewhere, Polly had read that the only social defense in this sort of situation is complete honesty.

Gathering her courage, she smiled sweetly at Mrs. Baines.

'Oh, it isn't *my* frock,' she said. 'It's Lady Windermere's.'

The marquis looked amused. 'You mean Mr. Oscar Wilde's Lady Windermere?' he asked.

'Yes,' replied Polly sedately. 'Act Two. I have a friend who was a theatrical dresser.'

All the gentlemen burst out laughing, including Mr. Baines, who received a fulminating glance from his wife.

Mrs. Baines did not know when she was defeated. 'And to say "the only female" is pure impertinence. *I* am here and all the other wives. There are plenty of ladies present.'

Polly's cool blue eyes drifted across the scene. 'You must forgive me, Mrs. Baines,'

44

she said gently. 'I really had not noticed.'

The marquis was beginning to feel heartily sorry for Mr. Baines. A shrew for a wife and a minx for a secretary.

'I am sure you must be looking forward to a cup of tea, Mrs. Baines. Why don't you take Miss Marsh over to the tables and your husband and I will refresh ourselves with something stronger,' he added with gentle malice, sliding his arm through the arm of the much gratified Mr. Baines.

'My Bert don't drink,' said Mrs. Baines.

Mr. Baines opened his mouth like a fish out of water.

'Oh, but we gentlemen have to discuss business. I insist,' said the marquis firmly.

'Don't worry about Miss Marsh,' said Lord Peter hurriedly. 'I'll escort her.'

He swept Polly off, leaving Gladys Baines alone with Sir Edward. Sir Edward's bad temper had returned. 'Harrumph!' he said to Mrs. Baines and stomped off.

The chatter at the tea tables stilled as Polly and Lord Peter approached. Amy Feathers, the switchboard girl, felt her heart sink right down to her little white spats. Bob Friend had been ever so attentive and now he was staring at that Polly girl as if no one else in the world

45

existed. The staff had been freely maligning Polly and her stuck-up ways in her absence and they, with the exception of Mr. Friend, felt it very unfair that, not only was she remaining unpunished for her cheek, but that she was being escorted to tea by a lord.

'I say, I don't feel like joining that mob,' said Lord Peter cheerfully. 'Hey, Jenkins. Fetch a little table over here under this tree for me and Miss Marsh.'

Jenkins brought a small card table over and spread it with a white cloth. He looked as if he would have liked to bundle Polly up in it and take her away and throw her in the lake.

Mrs. Baines glared across at Polly who was now seated tête-à-tête with Lord Peter. Polly's table under the spreading branches of a great oak tree looked deliciously cool, unlike the rest of the tables that were broiling in the sun. *If Bertie Baines doesn't dismiss that girl on Monday morning*, she thought, *I am going home to mother*.

'Where do you live, Miss Marsh?' Lord Peter was asking.

Polly thought desperately. She *knew* she belonged in this setting. What harm would a few lies do?

'I live with my foster parents in a quaint

little cottage near the City,' she said airily. 'They are very rough people, but honest. Old servants of my family, you know.'

'And your parents . . . ?'

'Oh, poor Mama and Papa. Such an unworldly couple. Never any money, you know. But they were great travelers. They were killed when I was just a baby. A typhoon . . . Indian Ocean, you know.' Here Polly produced a wisp of handkerchief and applied it to the corner of one dry blue eye.

'Oh, I say! I'm frightfully sorry. 'Course I knew you were good family the moment I saw you. Mama's a ridiculous snob. After all, Maisie Carruthers—you know, the Sussex Carruthers—is working as a stenographer. Secretary to Lady Jellings. Poor thing! Her family hasn't a bean and she lives in this businesswoman's hostel in Euston.'

Polly's brain was working overtime. Marriage to Lord Peter would be out of the question with the background of Stone Lane. But, now, an anonymous hostel for businesswomen!

'Is it very expensive?' she asked.

'What?'

'The hostel.'

'Can't be. Why?'

'I think it might be a good idea if I lived on my own,' said Polly slowly. 'I don't want to be a burden to my foster-parents ... poor old souls.'

Lord Peter's brain began to work as well. It would be one step nearer to having an affair with this dazzling girl if he could encourage her to leave home. Get her into the hostel and from there ... who knows ... a little maisonette in St. John's Wood?

'I say. If you're interested, I'll have a word with Maisie.'

'Thanks most awfully,' said Polly, looking into his eyes.

'Do you know, your eyes are the color of the summer sea,' he said.

'What a pretty compliment,' said Polly. 'But you are just flirting.'

He took her little gloved hand in his. 'I *never* flirt. I mean every word,' he said with boyish sincerity. Although he was only twenty, Lord Peter already had a small collection of broken hearts thanks to his air of boyish sincerity.

'*He's holding her hand*,' screamed the duchess, putting down a pair of binoculars. Her guests had left and she had just been joined by her elder son, the marquis.

'Edward! Go and tell Sir Edward that the picnic is finished and they all must go home. And tell Peter I want to see him *immediately*.'

'They're packing up anyway,' said her son indolently. 'But I shall fetch Peter for you.' The marquis was dressed in a white linen suit with a scarlet silk cravat. He looked cool and comfortable, unlike the poor members of Westerman's who had all put on their best frock coats and hard collars in honor of the occasion and were suffering accordingly.

He reached the tree with easy athletic strides and gave Polly a slight bow and a mocking look from under his heavy lids. 'Mama wishes to see you *immediately*, Peter.'

'Oh, rats! What does she want *now*?' said Peter crossly, getting to his feet. He had, however, just been sent down from Oxford for pouring bottles of champagne from the roof of New College onto the heads of the proctors below, and was still nervously awaiting his parents' decision as to his future.

'I'll drop in at Westerman's on Monday, Miss Marsh,' he said. 'And let you know'—here he glanced quickly at his brother—

'oh, well . . . I'll let you know about what we were talking about.' And with that, he ran away across the lawns.

The marquis stared down thoughtfully at the top of Polly's pink tulle hat. 'Since your cavalier has deserted you, Miss Marsh, may I escort you to the charabanc?'

Polly raised her head and the marquis looked startled. The girl was really incredibly lovely. 'Thank you, my lord,' she said quietly. He offered his arm and she rose and placed the tips of her pink kid-gloved fingers on it and moved across the lawn with him, her silk underdress making a soft swish-swishing noise on the grass. Polly tried to think of something to say to this awesome aristocrat. After all, he *was* going to be her brother-in-law. She glanced timidly up at the high-nosed profile but could think of nothing to say.

Oh, *how* she wished she had been able to afford to pay for that lovely brougham for the road back! The directors and their wives were leaving in their carriages. Even Mr. Baines had a little fly pulled by an overfed pony. But for the lower ranks the charabanc stood waiting, pulled by two enormous shaggy horses.

Polly turned to the marquis hesitantly
50

and held out her hand. 'Until we meet again, my lord,' she said softly.

He took her little hand in his and looked down at her thoughtfully. '*Are* we going to meet again, Miss Marsh?'

Her eyes flew to his face. 'But of course. I mean . . .' She fell silent.

*Oho!* thought the marquis. *So that's the way the land lies. Damn Peter! Philandering little monkey. The last time it had been that barmaid at Oxford, and now this!*

'Good-bye,' he said, firmly releasing her hand and turning abruptly away.

Polly climbed to the upper deck of the charabanc and sat down on the hard wooden seat next to Bob Friend and Amy Feathers. As the charabanc clattered down the drive, and the low branches of the trees began to brush the heads of the passengers on the upper deck, Polly took one long look back.

The duke and the duchess and their two sons were standing on the terrace. They seemed to be arguing.

*About what—about me?* wondered Polly. *I belong here!* she thought fiercely.

But as Mr. Oscar Wilde so rightly pointed out, 'All the world's a stage, but the players are badly cast.'

Polly turned back and settled herself down for the long journey home. She decided to practice her charm on Bob Friend and absolutely ruined what was left of the day for poor little Amy Feathers.

*    *    *

The staff picnic had left several of the travelers in cross and upset frames of mind.

Sir Edward Blenkinsop burst into his wife's boudoir in their Putney mansion, choleric blue veins standing out on his forehead.

'Women these days just don't know their place,' he began.

Lady Blenkinsop gave a delicate sigh and raised her Japanese fan to cover the look of boredom on her face. Lady Blenkinsop had been ill for as long as anyone could remember. Doctors could do nothing to cure her because there seemed to be nothing wrong besides an ever-present lethargy and general lack of spirits. She dragged herself from the bed in the morning, only moving as far as the chaise longue in her boudoir. She was a thin, faded woman in her forties.

'Do stop picking up things and putting

them down, Edward,' she said with a slight trace of animation. 'If you wish to complain about something, by all means complain and get it over with.'

Sir Edward needed only this cold encouragement. He burst forth with a long tale of the iniquities of Polly, ending up with '. . . and I shall see that she is dismissed first thing on Monday morning.'

'Oh, really, my dear,' said his wife in her quiet, frail voice. 'Do you consider that wise?' Lady Blenkinsop was beginning to feel interested in something for the first time in years. She had once met the Duchess of Westerman and had been terrified.

Imagine a little office girl taking in Her Grace like that!

'What d'ye mean "not wise"?' barked Sir Edward.

'Well, my dear,' said his wife plaintively, 'since this office girl seems to have enchanted young Lord Peter . . . I mean, wasn't there a rumor of Lord Peter going into the business after that scandal at Oxford?'

'Yes, of course. But what's that—'

'*And*,' pursued his wife with unaccustomed vigor, 'don't you think he

53

would be a little upset to find out that his *chère amie* had got the boot, so to speak?'

' "Got the boot!" Where do you pick up these common expressions? Pshaw. The duke would never stand for such goings on.'

'Oh no? What about that little actress from the Hippodrome who enjoyed the marquis's favors for some years? The duke didn't seem to mind.'

'If you mean Daisy Sharp . . . she was not employed by Westerman's.'

'But the duke *never* concerns himself with Westerman's,' said his wife sweetly. 'He told me so himself. Said trade was an awful bore.'

Sir Edward looked suspiciously at his wife from under his bristling eyebrows. 'Harrumph!' he said, taking a few more strides around the room and setting the pretty Dresden ornaments on the mantel jigging and bouncing.

He finally stopped his pacing and stood in front of his wife with his hands behind his back and his legs apart. 'Quite,' he said obscurely, staring at the carpet.

'So what will you do?' said his wife, raising herself up on one elbow.

'Well, well . . . harrumph. Do the

sensible thing. Turn a blind eye. Aristocracy has no morals,' said Sir Edward, who had paid for his knighthood.

His wife smiled faintly. 'I knew you would do what was right. But do let me know more about this Polly female.'

The eyebrows went up again. 'Good God, woman. Don't go concerning yourself about a female who is nothing more than a ... than ... a—a—*tart*.'

'Oh, absolutely,' drawled Lady Blenkinsop and sank back into her customary torpor.

★　　★　　★

Amy Feathers took off the black-and-white-striped poplin dress that she had worn to the picnic and hung it in a closet with sad, reverent movements of her thin, freckled arms. She could almost have been laying it to rest. She had had such hopes of that dress!

Before Polly had arrived, everything had been marvelous. Bob Friend and the other chaps from the office had teased her about how smart she looked. She had had quite a little court around her. Then Polly Marsh had arrived and they had all lost interest,

55

particularly Bob Friend, who had looked at Polly with a lost, hungry look.

Amy unfastened her Liberty bodice and popped her serviceable flannel nightgown over her head. How could any girl compete with someone as dazzling as Polly? But Polly had no eyes for Bob Friend ... only for that young Lord Peter.

All she could do, reflected Amy sadly, was wait until Polly Marsh had well and truly broken Bob Friend's heart and then, she, Amy, would be right on hand to pick up the pieces. Damn Polly Marsh, thought Amy, with unaccustomed venom. She hoped Lord Peter ruined her!

★　　★　　★

Polly and her mother were left alone in the kitchen in Stone Lane. The battle was over.

Polly had announced her decision to move to the businesswoman's hostel in Euston. Father Marsh had told his eldest daughter roundly that there was only one reason why single girls left home and had told Polly that one reason in very graphic terms. Then he had stomped off to the Prince Albert, Stone Lane's public house, to drink his fill with all the enthusiasm of the stag at eve.

Joyce had shouted at her, 'You ain't nuthin' but a rotten snob,' and had gone out, clutching little Alf, who was crying because of all the loud, angry voices. Through all the rumpus, Gran had carried on a long monologue about the shames and diseases that could befall any young maiden hell-bent on taking the primrose path, ending up with a lugubrious saga of a young girl called Rita who had once lived in Stone Lane and who had plunged into such a life of vice that ''er whatsit fell of.' She finally ambled off to bed after throwing her teeth, with a resounding clash, into a water glass by the sink.

Mrs. Marsh eyed her scarlet-faced daughter and took a deep breath. 'I'm a-lettin' you go, Pol. I knows why you're doing it. Cos you're ashamed of yer 'ome.'

'It's not that, Ma,' lied Polly desperately. 'I'd just like a bit of independence.'

'Well, let's hope you know wot to do wiff it,' said Mrs. Marsh heavily. She suddenly felt very old and her feet hurt.

'Remember this, my girl,' she said, struggling to her feet. 'The good Lord above ain't going to give you any more until yer learns to appreciate wot you've got.'

*　　　*　　　*

Hampstead Heath swam in the dusky blue twilight of a perfect summer's evening but Mrs. Gladys Baines was blind to its beauty. For once, the solid comfort of their villa overlooking the Heath with its heavy, highly polished mahogany furniture and dark, red plush portieres between the rooms did little to ease her anger.

She paced their sitting room with much the same lumbering, choleric gait as Sir Edward Blenkinsop, stopping occasionally to address the bald spot on top of her husband's bent head. Mr. Baines crouched forward in his armchair, miserably cracking his knuckles. 'For the last time,' grated his wife, 'why won't you get rid of that girl?'

'I've told you and told you,' sighed her husband. 'The girl is good at her job. The Westermans certainly seem to have forgiven her. It would cause an unnecessary fuss.'

'And that's your last word?'

'The last word on this subject, I hope,' said Mr. Baines meekly.

'Then, Bertie Baines, let me tell you this. I am going home to mother. And I am not returning until *that girl* is no longer employed in your office.' She rang the bell. A trim parlormaid appeared. 'Maisie, see that my things are packed,' said Mrs. Baines. Maisie bustled off with a crackle of starch and Mrs. Baines looked hopefully at her husband. He hadn't moved. She went slowly from the room and upstairs to supervise the packing.

When she descended some time later, he was still sitting as she had left him. Mrs. Baines tried again. 'I'm going, Bertie,' she said.

'Go if you must,' said Mr. Baines, getting to his feet, 'but I am not going to do anything that will jeopardize my position with Westerman's after all these years.'

His wife's answer was a monumental sniff of disdain. She swept out in a flurry of taffeta and, some minutes later, Mr. Baines heard the clop-clop of the carriage horses as they bore their infuriated burden off down the street.

Mr. Baines crouched back down in his chair. He felt immeasurably alone without his wife's domineering presence. The shadows were lengthening. He had been an utter fool. What was a chap supposed to do on his own? The heavy furniture seemed to be massing for the attack. 'You catch him on the left flank,' the table seemed to be saying to a hard, high-backed chair.

But the little imp who looks after henpecked husbands seemed to whisper in Mr. Baines's ear, 'A chap could take a nice promenade across the Heath on this beautiful evening. A chap could have a pint of mild and sit out over the pond at the Vale of Health pub and watch the ducks. A chap could . . .'

With a tremulous feeling of excitement, Mr. Baines hurriedly collected his tall silk hat and his best malacca cane. He pushed open the heavy, gloomy, stained-glass door, walked through the pocket-sized garden and stood for a moment on the pavement outside.

The gas lamps had been lit along the walk across the Heath and a faint mist had descended turning the lamps into great hazy, magic globes of light.

He walked across the road and ambled hesitantly along the walk. Above him, somewhere in the trees, a blackbird began to sing. 'Past your bedtime,' muttered Mr. Baines to cover the sudden rush of emotion he had felt at the bird's song. The greenish-blue misty light was turning to black and the lights of the pub were dimly reflected in the pond.

Above the pub door was a sign to tell all and sundry that the establishment had been licensed by George the Third for singing and dancing.

Slowly, Mr. Baines raised his cane and tilted his silk hat to a slightly rakish angle. He pushed open the glass doors and went in.

## CHAPTER FOUR

Miss Thistlethwaite's hostel for businesswomen could hardly be said to be a home away from home. As you pushed open the black, glossy door under the dingy Georgian fanlight, the mingled odors of strong tea, disinfectant, and dry rot rose around you.

The rooms were very small and barely furnished. An iron bedstead stood against the window that overlooked a sooty garden where no birds sang. There was a marble washstand against one wall and a curtained closet on the other. A minuscule round cane table ornamented the scuffed green

61

linoleum and a hooked rug lay beside the bed.

In the entrance hall two brass Benaras bowls of pampas grass formed a sort of dusty triumphal arch to a chilly sitting room, where a circle of hard-backed chairs held a perpetual conference.

All rules and regulations had been stitched in the form of samplers by an elderly relative of Miss Thistlethwaite's, who had tried to lighten their grim message by embellishing them with neatly stitched herbaceous borders. NO VISITORS IN THE ROOMS AT ALL TIMES. BATHS—TWO PENNIES. NO MALE VISITORS IN THE SITTING ROOM AFTER FIVE P.M. . . . and so on.

It was doubtful whether Polly would have been allowed a room had it not been for the departure of Lord Peter's friend, Maisie Carruthers, who confided to Polly, breathlessly, that she had been left a small legacy by an aunt and was going back to the country.

'You may have Miss Carruthers's room,' said Miss Thistlethwaite with a gracious creaking of stays and rustling of dusty black silk. 'You may move in your belongings as soon as Miss Carruthers moves hers out.'

Polly privately wondered *how* Miss

Carruthers was going to manage to move out. For an indigent gentlewoman she seemed to have a remarkable wardrobe of dresses. The tiny room was foaming with laces and silks and chiffons.

Maisie Carruthers was a thin, energetic girl of Polly's age with a large horselike face and bony red hands. 'Oh, bother!' she said, unstuffing a trunk for the hundredth time and looking wildly around. 'All this junk! Most of it's hand-me-downs from old jelly bag—Lady Jellings, I mean. She never wears a frock more than once.' She turned one dark eye on Polly. 'See here, if I leave you some money for the carter, could you be an angel and see that this stuff is shipped to the workhouse? I really don't want any of it. I *hate* clothes that are not my own, but Lady Jellings said I had to dress up because I was her social secretary.'

'I'll do it for you gladly,' said Polly, trying to keep the excitement from her voice and hoping Maisie would not guess that not one of these delicious confections would find its way to the workhouse.

'Oh, goody,' said Maisie. 'Then I can leave.'

She bent over to slam down the lid of her now nearly empty trunk and Polly held out her hands and hastily, with an imaginary measuring tape, took Maisie's measurements. The dresses would only have to be taken in a very little.

'Ta-ta,' said Maisie cheerfully. 'Oh, you'll find a gas ring in that whatsit by the fire. It pulls out. There's a law about no cooking in the rooms but we would all half starve if we obeyed it. I've got a frying pan and a plate and knife and fork hidden under the bed in a box. You're welcome to them.'

And, with a cheerful wave of her hand, and bumping her tin trunk enthusiastically against the bannister, Maisie Carruthers left.

Polly clasped her hands and took a deep breath as she looked at the sea of beautiful clothes. There were outfits for every social occasion. Nothing should stop her ascent up the social ladder now.

She began methodically to hang away the dresses. They would not all go into the closet but Maisie had hammered a line of nails into the wall and that sufficed to hold the rest of the hangers.

Polly cast her mind back to the days of the bewildering week before this Saturday morning when she had left home.

Contrary to her expectations and

everyone else's expectations, Mr. Baines had not given her a row. Instead, he had smiled at her and said that he hoped she had enjoyed her outing!

She had sailed through the Monday morning, typing letters energetically and waiting for the moment when Lord Peter would pop his head around the door. No one at all had appeared except that Amy Feathers, who had stood there silently, twisting her handkerchief between her fingers. When Polly had asked her what she wanted, Amy had burst into tears and rushed from the room.

Polly had been very chilly and aloof with Bob Friend, preferring to battle for her lunch herself every day. Then all too soon it was Thursday and there had been no sign of Lord Peter. In keeping with Polly's mood the weather turned nasty and chilly, and her fingers seemed to crawl across the gold and black keys of the typewriter. By lunchtime, she gave up hope. She had been eating penny mutton pies and saveloys for lunch all week, bought from the street vendor, to try to save her wages for her first week's rent at the businesswoman's hostel. Polly slammed down the wooden cover on her typewriter and determined to seek out

65

Bob Friend to join her for a one-shilling-and-sixpenny businessman's lunch. But it turned out that Bob had taken Amy Feathers, of all people, to lunch. Polly was just beginning to work up courage to pursue them to the chophouse when the door of her little office opened and there stood Lord Peter, shaking the raindrops from his black curls. It had all been arranged he said. Maisie would move out on Saturday, Polly would move in, and he, Peter, would take Polly for a drive in the park at three in the afternoon.

There was the sound of voices in the corridor outside and Lord Peter looked guilty and fled. But Polly's heart sang with happiness. A young man did not take a young lady driving in Hyde Park at the fashionable hour unless his intentions were honorable.

The morning then passed quickly and Polly decided to forgo lunch since Lord Peter had promised to buy her tea.

*　　*　　*

The Duchess of Westerman had had a busy morning as well. Directly after breakfast Sir Edward had called her and had informed her with awful coyness that Lord Peter had been at Westerman's. Did that mean Lord Peter was going to join the company or had he ... harrumph ..just been calling on that gel, Miss Marsh? Informing him acidly that she neither knew nor cared, the duchess had hung up the receiver and sent for her eldest son.

Edward, Marquis of Wollerton, was not at all surprised to hear what was troubling his mama. He had felt sure that Polly's name was bound to crop up sooner of later.

He found his mother in the morning room inexpertly trying to produce a flower arrangement out of several dried thistles and a piece of wood. 'Oh, drat the things,' she said as the marquis entered the room. 'It all looked *so* easy when that Jap did it at Nellie's party.'

The marquis surveyed it with interest. 'I suggest you glue it together,' he remarked languidly.

'Glue! Of course!' said the duchess, her brow momentarily clearing. 'Now, why didn't I think of that. Edward, you must help. Peter has been calling on that Marsh girl. He tells me that her parents were quite respectable people ... died in the Indian Ocean or something and only very respectable people do that. So he must be thinking of *marriage*. Quite out of the question. So you must go and buy her off.'

'Don't be such an utter chump, Mama,' said the marquis, raising his thin eyebrows. 'She doesn't belong to the demi monde. Not yet, anyway.'

'I wish to God she did,' said the duchess savagely. 'Look, Edward, I never ask you to do anything, do I? Please do this one little thing for me and stop Peter from getting entangled with that brazen hussy.' Her massive jaw trembled and her eyes began to fill with tears.

'Oh, very well,' said the marquis. 'I'll do it as much for the girl's good as for Peter's. Where shall I find her?'

'Here!' The duchess thrust a piece of paper at him. 'I found this in Peter's room. She's living in a hostel in Euston, but who knows how long *that* will last.'

'I'm going up to Town today,' said the marquis. 'I'll drop in on her. But there's not much I can do if Peter's really in love with her.'

'Balderdash!' said his mother. 'That sort of girl always has a price.'

★    ★    ★

Lord Peter strolled into the sitting room of the hostel and sat down on one of the hard upright chairs to wait for Polly. The sun slanted through the net curtains and shone on the row of aspidistras at the window. Outside, a small child was bowling his metal hoop to and fro on the sidewalk with monotonous regularity while a barrel organ wheezed out last century's music-hall tunes at the corner.

Lord Peter picked up a back number of *Country Life* and flicked through the pages until he found an article on polo. Just then the door of the small sitting room opened and he threw down his magazine and got to his feet. But it wasn't Polly. It was a small, fat woman with frizzy hair and twinkling blue eyes who was carrying two immense and bulging canvas shopping bags. *Must be the housekeeper or the cook*, thought Lord Peter, preparing to pick up his magazine again.

To his surprise, the newcomer plumped herself down next to him and breezily plunged into conversation with a cheery 'Ow are yer, ducks?'

'Very well, thank you,' said Peter, surveying the lady.

'Me dogs are barking,' said the good lady, easing off her shoes with a wince. 'It's them pavements, they gets harder the older ye get.'

Peter smiled noncommittally and picked up his magazine again, but the lady was still talking. 'Still, it'll be worff it to know my Pol 'as a decent bit o' food tucked away.'

Lord Peter raised his eyebrows. 'Pol?' he queried. 'Do you mean Miss Polly Marsh?'

'Yerse,' said the lady. 'Know my Pol?'

'I've come to take her for a drive,' said Peter. He introduced himself.

'Oh, so your Pol's lordship,' said Mrs. Marsh. 'Wot's this place like then?'

'I don't know,' said Peter faintly. 'Are you Polly's foster-mother?'

'Foster-mother! Naow! I'm Polly's ma. Wouldn't think it to see me now, would yer? 'Ere's me when I was Pol's age.'

She snapped open a capacious pinchbeck locket the size of a turnip. The hairstyle and dress were Victorian but the face was very like Polly's. Lord Peter grinned to himself. Parents drowned at sea, were they? What a rotten little snob Polly Marsh turned out to be. But all to the good. If she came from a cockney background, he had a better chance of seducing her, he thought

70

naively, unaware that the whole of Stone Lane was quite as likely to march him to the altar as any dowager.

'Anyway,' Mrs. Marsh went on, 'I've brought 'er some decent food. See these...' She opened one of her bulging bags and brought out a string of sausages. ''Ere ... take a sniff of these,' she said, holding them out to Lord Peter. 'Them's pure beef, them is. Not like some o' the muck they sells ahrand the West End where the toffs go.'

The door opened and Polly walked in and stood frozen to the spot.

Lit by the afternoon sunlight, Lord Peter's black curls were bent over a string of sausages held out by Mrs. Marsh that he dutifully sniffed. Polly was just about to turn and run when both looked up and saw her.

Lord Peter jumped to his feet. Polly opened and shut her mouth as she tried to think of what to say.

Her humiliation was about to be completed. The door behind her opened and Edward, Marquis of Wollerton, strode into the room.

His hooded eyes flicked from Peter, who was standing holding a string of sausages to the cheerful, smiling face of Mrs. Marsh.

Peter was grinning. 'I have not yet been formally introduced to this lady,' he said, waving a white hand toward Mrs. Marsh.

Polly gathered her wits together and performed the introductions with grace.

'Your *mother*,' said Lord Peter maliciously. 'I thought you said your parents were killed at sea.'

Mrs. Marsh's shrewd eyes roamed from Polly's distressed face to Lord Peter's malicious one. 'Oh, you're thinking of Uncle Albert,' she said cheerfully, ''im that was a stoker. Got washed overboard at Liverpool. That's who yer mean, isn't it ducks?'

Polly nodded gratefully but Lord Peter gleefully tried to bait her. 'But you said—' he began.

The marquis felt it was time to intercede. 'That's enough, Peter,' he said quietly. 'I was told you would be here and wish to discuss a matter of business with you but it can wait. Are you and Miss Marsh going anywhere?'

'Yes,' said Peter sulkily. 'I was going to take Miss Marsh for a drive.'

'Then don't let us keep you,' said the marquis languidly. 'Mrs. Marsh looks as if she could do with a strong cup of tea. Would you be my guest, Mrs. Marsh?'

'That would be luverly,' said Mrs. Marsh, lumbering to her feet and gratefully surrendering her heavy shopping bags into the marquis's hands. 'Take care of yerself, Pol. 'Ere! Wait a minute.'

Mrs. Marsh took in the full glory of her daughter's appearance. Polly was wearing Lady Jellings's rose silk gown. It was striped with inserts of rose velvet and she wore a shady rose velvet hat topped with large silk roses.

'That's about two hundred guineas you've got on yer back,' said Mrs. Marsh slowly, 'and I'd like to know where it came from.'

Polly blushed the color of her gown. 'Lord Peter's friend, Miss Carruthers, left me her wardrobe.'

'Hoh! That's all right, me girl. You had me worried for a bit,' said Mrs. Marsh with a hard look at Lord Peter.

'Come along,' said the marquis gently, taking Mrs. Marsh by the arm, 'and we'll leave these young things to enjoy their outing.'

'Ta, ever so, me lord,' said Mrs. Marsh. 'Good-bye, Pol. Be good.' She gave her

73

daughter a quick hug and a kiss and departed with the marquis. He helped her up into his carriage and then leaned forward. 'The Ritz, John, if you please.' Mrs. Marsh leaned back and heaved a sigh of pure pleasure.

*　　*　　*

To Polly's disappointment they did not go to Hyde Park but to St. James's. Hyde Park would be such a vulgar crush, said Peter, and Polly gloomily assented. All the fashionable world would be parading along the Row but she still felt too faint after her recent humiliations to protest. They left the carriage in Birdcage Walk and promenaded along beside the lake.

Polly stared unseeingly at the sunny water. She must say something.

'I'm sorry—very sorry about this afternoon,' she said with a rush. 'I lied about my parents.'

'That's all right,' said Peter. 'We all tell lies like that some time or another.'

*Not if your father's a duke, you don't,* thought Polly.

They halted at the railings to watch a family of ducks. Polly looked down and

74

realized that Peter had covered her gloved hand with his own and was pressing it warmly. 'Nothing you say or do could upset me, Polly,' he said in a low, intense voice. 'And I want you to call me Peter.'

'Peter,' said Polly shyly, glancing up at his handsome profile. This must be love . . . this heady feeling. She fought down the niggling voice at the back of her brain that was telling her that the thrill was caused by calling a young lord by his christian name.

He took her arm and they walked slowly on. 'I've got a bit of bad news, Polly,' said Peter. 'Father called at my diggings just before I left to meet you. I'm joining Westerman's—'

'But that's tremendous, Peter,' interrupted Polly. 'I shall see you every day.'

'Westerman's offices in Bengal,' he said gloomily. 'I won't be back home until Christmas.'

'Oh,' said Polly faintly.

'Buck up! It won't be all that long,' said Peter. He stopped and took a quick look around. They were under the shade of a stand of willows and nobody was near except an amorous guardsman chatting to a pretty nursemaid. Peter circled Polly's tiny waist and pulled her gently against him.

'We shall make the arrangements for our future at Christmas, Polly,' he said in a low voice. 'You know what I mean.'

'Yes. Oh, yes!' whispered Polly, envisaging a large wedding at St. George's, Hanover Square.

He bent his head and kissed her fleetingly and gently on the lips. *What a Christmas present*, he thought. *This lovely body in a little love nest in St. John's Wood!*

They smiled mistily at each other and walked on . . . unaware that their plans for the future were miles apart.

★   ★   ★

'So that's the way of it, me lord,' said Mrs. Marsh, putting down her teacup. 'Our Pol's done very well, coming from a place like Stone Lane. You can't blame the girl for a bit of snobbery. 'S'easy not to be snobbish if yer doesn't 'ave ter be.'

'True,' said the marquis, leaning back in his chair and eyeing Mrs. Marsh thoughtfully. 'Do you think Polly hopes to marry my brother?'

'Course!' said Mrs. Marsh. 'Stands to reason. Young 'andsome lord like 'im. Nuff to turn any young gel's 'ead.'

The marquis sighed. He had enjoyed Mrs. Marsh's company and her gossip about Stone Lane Market immensely and did not want to spoil the afternoon. But he felt it was his duty.

'My brother,' he said, 'is a thoughtless young bounder. I feel he doesn't plan to get married for a long time, if you take my meaning.' Gold eyes met blue for a long moment.

'Well, Pol won't settle for anything less than marriage, me lord,' said Mrs. Marsh. 'I wouldn't let her marry 'im anyways. No good comes of marrying out of yer class.'

'Oh, I wouldn't go as far as that,' said the marquis pleasantly. 'But certainly where Peter is concerned. He is going away, you know. To India. That should put a stop to his philandering.'

'Well, then,' said Mrs. Marsh brightening up. 'Wot's the two of us a-sittin' a-worryin' for. My Polly'll come to 'er senses soon enough. Thank you fer the tea, me lord. Oh, lord! 'S'all right, not you. I clean forgot to give Polly them sausages and things.'

'Peter will see that she is fed this afternoon, anyway,' said the marquis soothingly. 'I'll send you home in my carriage. I'm going to walk to my club.'

And so it was Mrs. Marsh and not Polly who dazzled Stone Lane by arriving in a carriage with a ducal crest on its side and two stunning footmen perched up on the back.

★    ★    ★

The marquis did not go to his club after all, but to his young brother's flat in Jermyn Street. He found Peter in great spirits, lying in a hot bath and drinking champagne.

'What's the celebration?' asked the marquis, perching himself on the edge of the tub. 'The loss of Miss Polly's virginity?'

'Not yet,' said Peter cynically. 'Pass the soap, there's a good chap. Yes, Polly. What on earth were you doing squiring old Mrs. Marsh?'

'I like her,' said the marquis simply. 'I don't want you to have an affair with young Polly, Peter. First of all, the girl's family is respectable—'

'Shoreditch! Respectable? Pooh!' said Peter rudely.

'I said respectable. Secondly, she works

78

at Westerman's.'

'Well, she'll have left Westerman's by the time I've got her to say "yes" to my evil designs,' said Peter cheerfully. 'What are you talking about and why are you worried about the girl's good name? She's working class and she's a rotten little snob—lied to me. Told me that'—here he mimicked Polly's voice—"Papa and Mama were drowned in the India Ocean. Typhoon, you know!" She's a stunning looker but take it from your baby brother, she's a common little tart with the soul of a slut and that's the way little Peter likes 'em.'

'I hope *you* get drowned in the Indian Ocean,' retorted the marquis. 'If I weren't sure that you would forget this nonsense by Christmas, I'd see to it that you were kept out there for longer.'

'I'm not a child,' said Peter sulkily. 'Go chase after your own love life.'

The marquis shrugged his elegant shoulders and left. He resolved not to trouble himself any more over Polly Marsh. The girl was obviously pretty hard-boiled and knew what she was doing. And Peter would definitely have cooled off before Christmas.

# CHAPTER FIVE

Lord Peter sailed away to India. At first
Polly received a few hurriedly scrawled
picture postcards that she faithfully pasted
into her album next to the Zena Dare
pictures. Then even the postcards ceased to
arrive.

Polly was not dismayed. It was not in the
nature of young men to write. Why, she
herself found it difficult to find the time to
pay as many visits to Stone Lane as she
should. For Polly was busy studying the
aristocracy.

She studied the grand ladies as they
alighted from their carriages at the theater
or in Bond Street, carefully noting their
dress and accents and listening to their
small talk. The world of the aristocracy as
portrayed in books and in the theater
showed her a world of witty, literate people
forever peppering their conversation with
quotations.

Polly plunged into an orgy of reading
until the world between the covers of a
book became more real to her than
anything outside. She would have liked a

friend to discuss her hopes and ambitions with, but she snobbishly did not want to encourage friendships with girls of the lower class and the upper strata were forbidden to her because of lack of money.

Religiously, she patronized the gallery of the opera or ballet, squeezing into her threepenny or fourpenny seat, avoiding the noisier vaudeville shows with their songs of lost, wonderful mothers, faithless sweethearts, and 'The Boys of the Old Brigade' that were secretly more to her taste.

There were eight other businesswomen in the small hostel. Polly only saw them at breakfast. The lady she shared a table with was as terrifyingly grand as a duchess and turned out to be none other than the silk buyer for Belham's. Polly had tried to strike up a conversation with the buyer who was called Miss Smythe and Miss Smythe had simply looked down her long thin nose and said, 'Beg poddon,' in such repressive tones that Polly had given up trying to be sociable.

Once, on one of her weekend visits to Stone Lane, she had passed a group of her former school-friends who were giggling and laughing and talking about boys. Polly had experienced a sudden pang of envy—a sudden longing to give up her ambitions, return to Stone Lane and merge with her background.

Her father, Alf, never ceased to voice his voluble disapproval—and as for Gran, she was quite convinced that Polly's smart clothes were being supplied to her by a series of lovers. Polly would have been horrified to learn that that illustrious director, Sir Edward Blenkinsop, was of the same opinion.

The Blenkinsops had rented a villa in Dinard for the month of August—not that the change of scene made any difference to Lady Blenkinsop, who had tottered from the vedette and, as soon as possible, established herself on a daybed in the sitting room, surrounded by her patent medicines and smelling salts and exuding an almost palpable atmosphere of boredom.

One morning, Sir Edward was standing at the sitting room window with his hands clasped behind his back. Even his hands looked angry, reflected his wife wearily, all chubby and red with great blue veins standing out on them.

'Tchah,' said Sir Edward, surveying the sunny scene. 'You should see what young

82

gels are wearing in the way of bathing dresses these days. Shocking!'

'Would you like to borrow my telescope, dear?' asked his wife with faint malice.

''Course not. What's come over you? These modern women. Take that Marsh girl at the office ... dressed like a duchess. She had a silk dress on before I left—silk!— and I'll swear it cost over two hundred guineas. Tart! Some masher's paying for her wardrobe, mark my words!'

'Perhaps she has some rich relatives,' said his wife.

'Not her! Family's pure cockney.'

'Still want to get rid of her?' queried his wife with the faint animation she only showed when the dreadful Miss Marsh's name was mentioned.

'Can't,' said her husband. 'Amy Feathers, the switchboard girl, told Mrs. Battersby, who does the cleaning, that Polly had received a postcard from Lord Peter. Mrs. Battersby told the message boy who told one of the clerks who told my secretary who told me.'

'Really, dear, what an old gossip you are!'

'Harrumph! Nonsense! Got to know the enemy. Spy chappies come in damned handy where there's a war.'

A thin smile of amusement curled Lady Blenkinsop's pale lips. 'And is there war at Westerman's?'

. 'Of course there is! Can't have office girls stepping out of their class. That's Bolshevism!' He laid one finger along his nose and leered at her awfully. 'Old Blenkinsop has his ear to the ground.'

'And his eye to the keyhole,' said his wife, abruptly losing interest.

'But mark my words,' went on Sir Edward, 'nothing will come of her ambitions. Lord Peter is an impressionable young man but his elder brother will soon put a stop to any shenanigans.'

★　　★　　★

The elder brother had, in fact, dismissed the matter of Polly from his mind. He had just received a letter from Peter, who seemed to be head over heels in love with the Honorable Miss Jane Bryant-Pettigrew, daughter of Colonel, Sir Percy Bryant-Pettigrew, at present stationed in India. The duchess was ecstatic. A respectable marriage was just what Peter needed to settle him down and the manager of the

Bengal office had reported that Peter was *working*, actually working, which all went to show what the influence of a good woman could do.

The marquis was strolling through Shepherd's Market on his way to his club one fine Saturday in autumn. There was an exhilarating tinge of cold in the sunny air. Huge bunches of chrysanthemums stood in tubs outside the florists and a faint smell of roast chestnuts scented the sooty air.

An organ-grinder was churning out 'Tales from the Vienna Woods' with relish while his little red-capped monkey nipped nimbly in and out of the crowd, rattling its cup with all the verve of a professional beggar.

The marquis stopped with the crowd to watch the little animal's antics. Then out of the corner of his eyes he noticed a group of rough-looking youths over by the chestnut-seller.

They had heated a penny until it was red hot and with one deft motion of the tongs, one of them threw it toward the monkey. Everything seemed to happen in a flash. There was a groan of dismay from the crowd as the monkey nipped forward eagerly to catch the burning-hot penny.

Then, as the coin was in midair, a very beautiful girl leaped from the crowd and caught the coin in her gloved hand and, seizing her umbrella, ran to the group of youths and began beating them soundly about their heads.

The monkey's rescuer was none other than Miss Polly Marsh.

The youths had recovered from their shock and showed every sign of fighting back. The crowd was cheering Polly noisily.

The marquis stepped forward and put his arms around the enraged Polly and dragged her away from the youths. She twisted angrily in his arms and looked up only to see the lazy mocking eyes of the Marquis of Wollerton looking down into her own.

'Please be calm, Miss Marsh,' he begged, releasing her. 'They will not try that trick again . . . at least not today.'

'Wretches!' said Polly.

He noticed that one gloved hand was clenched into a fist and gently opened the fingers. The red-hot coin had burned a hole in her glove and a blister was already beginning to form on her palm.

'You must have that attended to, Miss Marsh,' he said gently. 'We are only a step from Brown's Hotel. They serve an excellent tea there and I can find someone to attend to your hand. Would you care to join me?'

Would she care to join her future brother-in-law? 'Of course,' said Polly with a radiant smile. He hailed a passing four-wheeler and ushered Polly in. The enthusiastic crowd gave the monkey-rescuer three hearty cheers as the carriage pulled away, and Polly grinned and waved.

The marquis looked at her thoughtfully. When she wasn't trying to be a correct young lady, there was something very young, vulnerable, and endearing about Miss Marsh. Then he noticed her frock and his thin black brows snapped together. Polly was wearing a smart walking dress of scarlet velvet, cut with the hand of an expert. Now where, mused the marquis, had Miss Marsh managed to afford to buy a frock like that?

Brown's Hotel in Albemarle Street was quickly reached and while Polly was having her hand bandaged, he ordered afternoon tea and looked forward to solving the mystery of Miss Marsh.

Polly soon entered cheerfully to join him. Brown's Hotel was not nearly as terrifying as she had expected, more the way she fancied a pleasant country house would be with its charming little rooms, wood-paneled walls, and cheerful fires crackling away to dispel the autumn chill.

She busied herself with the teacups with all the professional ease of a West End hostess and then settled back and looked inquiringly at her escort. 'Have you heard from Peter?' she asked shyly and then blushed in case the marquis would think the use of his brother's christian name too familiar.

'I heard only the other day,' he said. 'Peter seems to be working hard, which is unusual.'

'I had several postcards from him,' said Polly brightly, helping herself to a watercress sandwich.

The marquis, who did not know that Polly had not received a postcard for some time, silently cursed his brother.

To change the subject, he questioned her about her work at Westerman's, and then baldly asked her how much she earned.

'I now earn fifteen shillings a week,' said Polly proudly. 'Mister Baines gave me a raise.'

The temptation was too much. 'How

then,' said the marquis, 'can you afford that very charming dress you are wearing?'

Polly's face hardened. 'If you will cast your mind back, my lord, perhaps you will remember that I informed my mother that I had inherited Miss Carruthers's wardrobe. Even in Shoreditch your questions about my salary and my clothes would be considered impertinent!'

'You must forgive me,' said the marquis, smiling into her eyes in a way that suddenly made her feel breathless. 'My friends will tell you that I am terribly rude.'

Polly looked at him cautiously. He did not seem nearly so terrifying when he smiled like that. She said, laughing, 'Don't do it again or I might hit you with my umbrella. And it would never do to strike my future brother-in-law, you know. Oh, look! They have *madeleines* on the second tier. I love *madeleines*.'

'Very fattening,' he said lightly, while his brain recovered from the shock.

Polly laughed again. 'Not nearly so fattening as those éclairs on the top. I've never seen such huge—why are you looking at me like that?'

The marquis sighed. 'Your announcement—that is your remark that I was to be your brother-in-law—startled me. Did Peter actually *propose* marriage?'

'Yes,' said Polly, and then hesitated. 'Well . . . that is . . . he said almost the same thing. He said that he would return at Christmas and that we would make plans for our future together. What else does that mean, if not marriage?'

'My dear,' said the marquis slowly, 'in Peter's language, it probably means a maisonette in Saint John's Wood.'

'Oh,' said Polly, relieved. 'But you must not worry. Saint John's Wood is a very pretty suburb, and although a maisonette may not seem very grand to you—'

'My dear girl,' snapped the marquis, 'by Saint John's Wood, I mean that Peter is suggesting setting you up in a love nest as his mistress.'

He watched the painful blush spreading over Polly's face and cursed himself. Why, the girl was innocent! Contrary to what was portrayed in current romances, the modern young lady seemed to have forgotten how to blush.

'How cruel you are,' said Polly in a whisper. 'How cruel and *snobbish*. You are just like your awful mother. Duchess, indeed! She behaved exactly like these stuck-up shopgirls I meet at the hostel and you, my lord, are no better. Peter loves me. He . . . he *kissed* me.'

The marquis groaned. 'Miss Marsh. You are indeed a very kissable girl. But Peter is practically engaged to some girl out in Bengal.'

Polly looked at him in dismay. Then her vanity came to her rescue. She had never met any girl or any woman who was as beautiful as herself.

'Tommyrot!' she said roundly, gathering up her gloves and reticule. 'You're ashamed of me, that's all!'

He politely got to his feet. 'I am not in the least ashamed of you, Miss Marsh,' he said in chilly accents. 'I think you are ashamed of yourself. Furthermore, I don't believe you love my brother one little bit.'

'Oh!' gasped Polly, outraged. 'You pompous *old* windbag. Just because *you* were disappointed in love . . .'

She raised her hand to her mouth realizing she had indeed gone too far. The marquis's face was a mask of distaste.

'Allow me to find you a cab, Miss Marsh. I am sorry to cut short our engagement but I have an appointment at my club.'

'*You* didn't cut it short. *I* did,' snapped

the irrepressible Polly and swept out, leaving him standing over Brown's best afternoon tea, feeling like an utter fool.

★ ★ ★

Had the marquis been less annoyed he might have realized the folly of confiding in his mother. He was very fond of his mother, although most of the time he did not like her one bit.

On the Sunday, he strode into his mother's boudoir unannounced, wishing for the hundredth time that the duchess would say good-bye to the 1880s, although he had to admit grudgingly that her boudoir was the only room in the Chase where the twentieth century was not allowed to intrude. The sunny day was shielded from the room by crimson-and-green rep curtains inside and the tendrils of ivy outside, which created a sort of tropical underwater effect in which swam large round tables surrounded by massive books and wax flowers under glass.

His mama was dealing with her correspondence, dressed in a dirty lace tea gown that was cut low at the back to show an acreage of mottled and unwashed neck.

'Edward,' she cried, turning and kissing the air about a yard from his face. 'You look very grim. What's the matter?'

'Miss Marsh,' said the marquis heavily and immediately wished he had not opened his mouth.

'Oh, no!' cried the duchess. 'Not you, Edward. I'm so delighted that Peter is showing such sense.'

Wearily, the marquis told her of his afternoon tea with Polly and of Peter's dishonorable intentions.

'Well!' said the duchess, breathing a sigh of relief and then looking rather shifty. 'After all, what a lot of fuss about nothing. How *Victorian* you *are* being, Edward. After all, one knows that simply scads and scads of people these days have mistresses. I mean, you yourself—'

'I do not seduce virgins or innocent girls,' said her son coldly, 'and I believe Miss Marsh to be both. Furthermore,' he added, holding up his hand, as his mother would have spoken, 'she comes from a very respectable family. I have had tea with her mother.'

'*Really*,' said his mother, outraged. 'There are a lot of times, Edward, when we do not see eye to eye, but until now I have

93

never known you to have a penchant for fraternizing with the lower orders.'

The marquis felt himself becoming very angry indeed. 'You're a snob, Mama,' he said curtly. 'Unfortunately what Polly Marsh said about you seems to be true. You are exactly like a snobbish shopgirl!'

'She *dared* to say that!' screamed the duchess. 'Then if you didn't slap her face for her cheek, I am going up to town tomorrow, going straight into Westerman's, and I am going to do it myself!'

The marquis regarded her thoughtfully. 'Do, by all means, Mama, but everyone will think, first, that you're frightfully common and, second, that Peter means to marry Miss Marsh and that you are jealous.'

The duchess breathed heavily. 'Then I shall see that she's fired.'

'Equally common,' said her son, who by now had his temper well in check. 'Anyway, if you do, I shall make a *very* funny story about it and tell it round the clubs.'

'You wouldn't *dare*!'

'Try me . . . as our American cousins would say.'

'I shall speak to your father.'

'Do. But it won't do any good, you know. He prefers to go on as if Westerman's doesn't exist. He hated that picnic, you know. It was all Blundell's idea.' Blundell was the duke's secretary.

The duchess gave her elegant son a withering look but could think of nothing to say, and so she began to cry. Her ability to burst into tears on any occasion had pierced the hearts of her admirers when she was a pretty debutante. She could never understand why it now made strong men run for cover but it was her favorite weapon and she still exercised it on all occasions.

When she finally dried her eyes, it was to see, with intense irritation, that her son had fled.

She racked her brains for a weapon to use against the impertinent Miss Marsh. A bottle of smelling salts on her table winked at her in the greenish gloom. She had it! Edward Blenkinsop's wife! She would call on her without delay and enlist her help.

*     *     *

Lady Blenkinsop looked at her butler with utter dismay. 'The Duchess of Westerman? Are you sure?'

'Yes, my lady.'

'Oh, very well, I suppose I had better see her. Bring us some tea, Wilkins, and some of those little *choux* pastry things of cook's.'

Lady Blenkinsop raised herself from the chaise longue and then sunk back again. Illness was sometimes a very good defense.

The duchess sailed into the room bringing with her the strong smell of gardenia talcum powder, acrid sweat, and the added smell of something which Lady Blenkinsop's maiden aunt would have designated as 'much worse.'

'My *dear* Lady Blenkinsop. Please do not get up. I myself know what it is to be frail and exhausted.' As indeed the duchess, who was prey to monumental hangovers, certainly did. 'I am sorry to arrive so unexpectedly but I really must have your help. It's about the Marsh girl.'

'Indeed!' Lady Blenkinsop found the energy to sit up. 'You must tell me *all* about it, Duchess,' she crooned sympathetically.

Wilkins entered at that moment with a tea trolley laden with the pastry cook's art. The tea was vulgarly strong and Indian. The duchess began to think that Lady Blenkinsop was really a very, very sympathetic and intelligent woman.

She poured out her story the minute Wilkins had left, ending up with Polly's infernal cheek, calling her a shopgirl, indeed, and how it looked as if Edward were smitten.

A faint flush of color rose to Lady Blenkinsop's pallid cheeks and she tried not to smile. Whatever else Polly Marsh might be, she was certainly no toady.

But she murmured sympathetically, 'My poor Duchess. What can one do? Sir Edward informs me that Mrs. Baines has left Mister Baines because he refuses to dismiss Polly, and the wicked Mister Baines is so delighted with his bachelor life that he has given the girl a raise. In fact, he lives in terror of her leaving in case his wife comes back to him!'

'No! Fancy!' gasped the duchess, slurping her tea.

'Yes. Fancy!' said Lady Blenkinsop, reflecting that Miss Marsh did give one a new slant on life. The duchess, for example, would certainly be classed as common were she not a duchess. And good God! The woman badly needed a bath.

Lady Blenkinsop pretended to be thinking deeply. After some minutes she said in her gentle, tired voice, 'I think your fears are groundless, Duchess. You must know that Edward is not at all susceptible. And now you tell me that Peter is as good as engaged!'

'True,' snapped the duchess. 'But I would like that little upstart's pretensions depressed.'

Lady Blenkinsop was overcome by a desire to meet the intriguing Miss Marsh and she suddenly saw a way in which it could be managed.

'I would not do this for just anyone,' she began, 'but I would like to help you. I shall invite Miss Marsh to tea. She has not been in the habit of socializing with ladies of our quality. I feel sure that I can persuade her that she would not "fit in."'

'Most obliged to you,' said the duchess, 'but couldn't I do that myself?'

'By no means,' said Lady Blenkinsop firmly. 'Miss Marsh would *expect* you to be antagonistic. Please leave it to me.'

'Grrumph,' assented the duchess, her mouth crammed with pastry.

★　　★　　★

Polly stared at the embossed card, her blue eyes wide with fright. Tea! With Lady

Blenkinsop, Saturday, October First. What was it all about? Should she go?

* * *

Tea! Lady Blenkinsop! The marquis turned the card over in his long fingers. Why on earth had she invited him? He did not feel like traveling all the way to Putney to take tea with a lady whom he had met once and classed as a professional invalid. Should he go?

## CHAPTER SIX

The Blenkinsops' large Victorian villa in Putney was called Mandalay, turreted and gargoyled on the outside and suffocatingly overfurnished and overheated on the inside. Formal gardens, now bare of flowers, ran down to the edge of the steel-gray Thames.

Timidly pushing open the great iron gates, Polly wished for the umpteenth time that Maisie Carruthers had been employed by Lady Jellings in winter as well as summer. All the glory of the cobweb-lace tea gown was at the moment eclipsed by a shabby and worn plaid mantle of her own. Still, the butler would hopefully take that away and hang it in some dark closet before any of the company saw her. She wondered how many other guests had been invited. There were no carriages standing at the front of the house but then, she felt sure that she was early by about ten minutes.

Wilkins relieved her of the shabby mantle and then led the way through a large dark hall that was an indoor jungle of pampas grass in Benaras brass bowls, reminding Polly suddenly of the entrance to the sitting room at the hostel.

'Her ladyship,' said Wilkins, 'will be with you presently.' He held aside the heavy red portiere and Polly stepped into the sitting room.

Sir Edward Blenkinsop rose to meet her.

Now, as far as Lady Blenkinsop was concerned, Sir Edward had already left to play a round of golf. But the bold Sir Edward had decided to linger behind to try his luck with the 'ladybird.' The girl was no better than she should be, despite her clothes and airs. And he, Sir Edward, had been considered a bit of a dandy in his youth, and damme, if he was sure he hadn't lost the old Blenkinsop touch.

Twirling his shaggy gray mustache like a stage villain, Sir Edward advanced on the startled Polly. 'Well, well, well, Miss Marsh! By Jove! Well, well, well...'

Not a very sparkling conversational opening but Sir Edward was unaware of it. Inside, his voice was teasing and flirting and saying all sorts of deliciously naughty things. He was amazed that she did not fall into his arms. Instead, she sat down nervously on a red plush chair, perching herself on the edge of it as though ready for flight. 'Well ... Ha! Ha! ... yes, yes, yes ... well, well, well ...' giggled Sir Edward while inside his soul rollicked and rolled. 'By Jove!' he added in an intense whisper and bending forward, he placed one fat hand on Polly's knee. He was panting and chuffing and blowing through his mustache. There! He hadn't lost the old touch.

Polly stared as if mesmerized at the 'old touch' on her knee and at the fat blue veins like worms, which throbbed and bulged like separate creatures.

The door opened and Lady Blenkinsop, followed by the Marquis of Wollerton, walked into the room and froze at the sight of her husband.

'Edward! Leave this house immediately.'

'It's my house,' said Sir Edward childishly.

'It's mine,' snapped Lady Blenkinsop, as indeed it was. She looked thoughtfully at her husband as he crawled from the room. 'Edward!'

'My dear.'

'Edward Blenkinsop, you are a *masher*!'

The change in Sir Edward was ridiculous. He immediately puffed and swelled with pride like a bullfrog. 'You'll be beggin' me to come back, Jennie, see if you don't. I'll be at my club.'

He slammed the door so hard that the draft blew the heavy red portiere back and forth and set its fringe of bobbles dancing.

'You must forgive my husband,' said Lady Blenkinsop, looking quite healthy from her exertions. 'And forgive me also for making such a scene but, you see,' she added, 'I simply couldn't bear the sight of the man any longer.'

If the duchess had meant Polly to be cowed by Lady Blenkinsop's manner, it certainly was succeeding—if 'being cowed' meant being more embarrassed than you have ever been.

Lady Blenkinsop sank gracefully into a chair and looked at Polly affectionately. 'Poor girl! How badly I am behaving and how embarrassed you must be. But when I came into the room and saw Edward with his hand on your knee, it all came over me in a flash. Mister Baines, I thought. You see Edward told me that Mrs. Baines left Mister Baines because he would not dismiss you, and Mister Baines is having such a jolly time as a bachelor that he lives in fear and dread of your departing the firm.'

'Oh!' cried Polly in distress, covering her red face with her hands.

'I was dying to meet you, which is why I invited you to tea, but I never thought for a minute that it would work out so splendidly. Ah, Wilkins. Tea. Just leave the things and go. Now we can be comfortable!'

The marquis felt great pity for the distressed Polly. He was too used to the direct speech and eccentricities of various society ladies to be embarrassed but he realized it must indeed be a new experience for Miss Marsh. He launched into a light description of all the gossip and affairs of society until he noticed that Polly was looking more composed.

Polly really did not know what to make of her hostess. And she dismally remembered her last encounter with the marquis and all those horrible lies he had told her about Peter.

She suddenly realized that the marquis had stopped talking and that Lady Blenkinsop was addressing her. 'Now, Miss Marsh, I believe you live in Stone Lane in Shoreditch and that there is a weekly market there. Tell me all about it.'

Polly stiffened, but Lady Blenkinsop's kind face was alive with interest. Polly began to slowly describe the Sunday market, the noise, the bustle, the friendliness, the feuds between the traders, which were quickly forgotten once the market was closed. Lady Blenkinsop listened intently and begged for more. Still in a hesitant voice, Polly began to describe her family and surroundings, suddenly finding it a relief to be absolutely honest. Her voice growing stronger, she told of Joyce's addiction to comics, her father's terrible threats that he never meant or carried out, and of Ma's comfortable kitchen and her ability to produce splendid hot meals at the drop of a hat. Lady Blenkinsop drank it all in with the air of someone greedy for life and the marquis watched Polly's beautiful and animated face and thanked his lucky stars that he was a confirmed bachelor. The girl was enough to bewitch anyone!

When Polly had finished, Lady Blenkinsop sat back with a sigh. 'How marvelous. How *alive!*' she breathed. 'I think that perhaps with Edward gone I shall be able to go out and about a little more. Edward always intimidates me and makes me feel ill, you know. I can never seem to carry on a conversation without him harrumphing and barking and saying, "I don't understand the rubbish you talk. I'm a plain, simple soldier and I like things said in plain, simple terms."'

She rose to her feet. 'Now, if you will both forgive me, I must rest. My dear Marquis, will you be so kind as to escort Miss Marsh back to town? You will? Splendid! Come, give me a kiss, my dear, and call on me at any time.'

After they had left, Lady Blenkinsop went slowly upstairs. She had not enjoyed herself so much in a long time. She thought fleetingly and guiltily of the duchess. Well, she hadn't meant to humiliate the girl anyway; simply to meet her. And she had asked the marquis in order to discover whether he was enamored of Polly. But the marquis's face had been like a well-bred mask. Pity! They made such a handsome pair.

Then she gave a happy chuckle as she thought of her banished husband and rang the bell to tell Wilkins to tell the cook to take every grain of curry powder in the kitchen and throw the stuff on the garbage heap. Sir Edward would not be dining at home again. Not if she could help it.

★    ★    ★

The marquis and Polly traveled a good length of the way back to the center of London in chilly silence. Polly was still furious with him for his disparaging remarks at Brown's and for his part, the marquis thought sourly that the girl was too attractive for her own good.

At last, as the horses were clopping toward Euston, some imp forced him to say, 'Still expecting to marry my brother, Miss Marsh?'

'Of course,' said Polly, turning her head to stare out of the window. 'A gentleman doesn't kiss a lady unless he means to marry her.'

'Don't be so naive,' drawled the marquis. 'If all the men married all the girls they'd kissed, we'd have polygamy all over the country. A kiss means nothing. It's simply a pleasant gallantry that leads to ... well, never mind.'

She looked at him with slightly disdainful and inquiring surprise, the light of a gas lamp shining on her gold curls, making her large eyes great black pools of mysterious depths.

He swore gently and pulled her toward him. She stared as if mesmerized at the white high-nosed face bending over her and the thin, mobile mouth coming closer to hers.

His thin, cool lips pressed gently against hers, much as Peter's had done, and then pressed closer as his tongue gently parted her mouth. And then all the skyrockets and Catherine wheels and Roman candles burst and rocketed across a sky of deep black velvet.

The carriage came to a stop. Polly wrenched herself from his arms, stumbled from the carriage, and ran into the hostel.

The marquis sat as still as a statue, staring straight ahead, his eyes hooded by his heavy lids and his chin sunken into his fur coat while his carriage rumbled over the cobblestones toward the West End of London.

## CHAPTER SEVEN

The November gales whistled and roared through the twisting streets of the City, swept up the Strand to Leicester Square, scampered along the Tottenham Court Road and, howling along Goodge Street and increasing in force by the minute, plunged into Euston and tore slates from the roofs, sent chimney pots flying and sent whirlwinds dancing around the arch of Euston Station.

Polly Marsh was worried. She rose shivering and tiptoed across the icy linoleum to the washstand in the corner. The water in the ewer had a small film of soot on it as the gale seemed to have forced the output of London's chimneys through every crack in her small room.

Lord Peter Burley had not written. He had not replied to her many letters although she had kept them light, gossipy, and friendly, and had not mentioned anything about their future together.

Westerman's was to have its first Christmas party ever, and Polly had dreamed of announcing her engagement before that time and then gracefully retiring from the grubby world of commerce. She had tossed and turned all night in her narrow bed, dreaming endlessly of walking in St James's Park with Lord Peter. But every time he bent his head to kiss her, his face faded to be replaced by that of the marquis. And what was even more horrible about these dreams was that she was always glad it was the marquis instead of Lord Peter.

She carefully put on the scarlet velvet dress that was now smelling strongly of benzine from repeated cleanings. Her precious store of rice powder was nearly finished. Polly sighed. Perhaps if she managed to slip a few pieces of toast from the breakfast table into her reticule, she would make them do for lunch and save the money toward a new box of powder. She had told Mrs. Marsh not to bring any more food parcels and her mother had good humoredly agreed. Polly had not wanted the other girls to see her cockney mother arriving with shopping bags of groceries. So now there was no store of biscuits and sausages hidden in her small cupboard next to the gas ring.

She went down to the small dining room and sat down at her allotted table. The Belham's buyer was already there, studying the social column of *The Times*. Polly eyed Miss Smythe under her lashes, waiting for a chance to thieve some pieces of toast when the beady eye of the buyer was otherwise employed. She had just seized three pieces of toast and, under cover of the tablecloth, was about to slip them into her reticule, when Miss Smythe let out a startled exclamation and put down the paper.

'Beg poddon,' she began. 'Eh believe you know Lord Peter Burley.'

Polly nodded dumbly, her nervous fingers clutching the buttered toast.

'Eh see he has just become affianced to a lady in Bengal ... a Miss Jane Bryant-Pettigrew.'

'Nonsense!' said Polly. The toast fell unheeded to the carpet.

Miss Smythe bridled. 'Beg poddon, miss. Look here.'

She held out the paper and Polly took it in her buttery fingers. There it was at the top of the social column in black and white. Lord Peter Burley had indeed become engaged to Miss Jane Bryant-Pettigrew, daughter of Colonel, Sir Percy Bryant-Pettigrew.

The room seemed to swim around her. Miss Smythe's voice, saying crossly, 'You hehve put bottor on meh pepah,' seemed to come from a long way away.

Mumbling something incoherent Polly fled from the room, and, slipping on her old coat, hurtled out into the windy street, oblivious of the gale. The turmoil of the storm as she made the long, long walk from Euston to the City was nothing compared to the turmoil in her brain.

How could he? What would she tell her family? How they would be laughing at her in the office, thought poor Polly, unaware that the office staff had already forgotten her noble friendship long, long ago.

It was all the fault of that sneering brother of his, decided Polly at last, as she negotiated the crowded pavements of Fleet Street and battled the cross winds at Ludgate Circus. He had *forced* poor Peter to become engaged to Miss Jane Bryant-Pettigrew. All the way up Ludgate Hill Polly cursed the marquis in her mind. She was in such a rage that she did not realize that it would be very difficult for the marquis to force his brother to marry anyone when he, the marquis, was in England and Lord Peter in India. By the time she reached St. Paul's Polly suddenly felt very young and weak and vulnerable. She did not know whether or not to go into church and pray. Pray for what? Perhaps God felt that little office girls should keep to their own caste. With the wind whipping the salt tears from her cheeks, she finally pushed open the door of Westerman's.

For the first time she was glad of her isolated cubicle away from the gossip and noise of the main office. She needed a plan of action. Lady Blenkinsop! *She* would know what to do.

The long morning of letters and invoices dragged on, the clatter of the typewriter keys accompanied by deep rumblings from Polly's stomach. She even thought longingly of the crushed toast lying on the carpet back at the hostel. Near lunchtime her door opened and Bob Friend popped his curly head around the edge. For a long time after the office picnic he had not come near Polly, but lately he had begun to drop into her office with every sort of excuse.

'Hey, Miss Marsh,' he said. 'Care to join me for a spot of lunch? I won a whole five pounds at a bridge party last night. Please say you'll let me treat you.'

Polly opened her mouth to give a chilly refusal but her stomach was rumbling and her heart was sore. 'All right, Mister Friend,' she said suddenly, 'I'd love to.'

'Oh, jolly good,' said a radiant Bob. 'I'll come back for you in ten minutes.' He went off down the corridor whistling to himself and nearly collided with Amy Feathers. Amy looked up at him shyly. 'Are you having lunch with me today, Bob?' Amy had been bringing a generous lunch basket to the office during the past few months and Bob had got into the habit of sharing it with her in her little room upstairs where she worked at the switchboard. He had never asked her to go out with him, but Amy was happy with her lunches and lived for them. She spent a whole weekend planning tasty menus.

Bob looked at her and blushed guiltily. Amy was the one he should be taking for lunch. 'I—I can't, Amy,' he stammered. 'I promised to take a friend for lunch; old school pal.'

'That's all right, Bob,' said Amy shyly. 'I

113

don't mind. There's always tomorrow.'

'Oh, yes ... what. Certainly,' said poor Bob, edging past her and praying that Amy would never find out about his lunch with Polly.

But the gods were not on his side. Amy had been so disappointed that she had decided to take a short walk before eating her lunch. The wind was so fierce and so cold that she had only taken a few steps when she changed her mind and turned to reenter the office, subsequently getting a splendid view of Bob Friend escorting Polly Marsh to the chophouse, looking every bit as if it were Christmas already.

Amy trailed miserably through Westerman's. In her mind, Polly was worse than Delilah. She had turned that fine, upstanding young man, *her* Bob, into a *liar*. But although her eyes were slightly blurred with tears, Amy was still able to make out an imposing-looking letter with a foreign stamp lying in the post basket. She wiped her eyes and picked it up. Yes, she had been right! It had a Bengal postmark and was addressed to Miss Polly Marsh. Now shrewd little Amy had heard all about Lord Peter's engagement and knew exactly why the usually standoffish Polly had suddenly decided to have lunch with Bob Friend.

Well, she would just see if this letter could possibly spoil that charming little lunch. Amy was not a vindictive girl; only very much in love.

★    ★    ★

What an utterly marvelous thing hot food was! Only a half an hour ago Polly Marsh could have sworn that she had not long to live, torn as she was between the torments of rage and jealousy. Now as the last spot of marmalade pudding, dripping with hot custard, was popped into her pretty mouth, she felt as if she would live to fight another day.

As for Bob Friend, he was so enraptured with his companion that Amy had to cough twice before he looked up. Amy could not resist saying, 'I didn't know you and Miss Marsh were old school friends.'

Bob blushed and murmured something incoherent into his pint of mild. 'Anyway,' Amy went on, 'I'm sorry to interrupt your lunch but I've got a letter for Miss Marsh and I thought it might be important.'

She held out the Bengal letter to Polly. To her fury, Polly only glanced at it and said, 'Thank you, Amy,' in a condescending tone of voice. Amy hesitated, looking appealingly at Bob, hoping he would ask her to sit down. But Bob was too embarrassed to do more than study the remains of his marmalade pudding as if he thought it was the most fascinating thing on earth. Amy gave a jerky nod of her head and puffed out her small bosom like a midwinter sparrow and then walked away.

Polly's heart was hammering but she was not anxious to open the letter. It would contain nothing but excuses and apologies—of that she was sure. Bob eyed her sadly. Polly's face was like a mask and all her bright interest in him had fled. He miserably paid the bill and escorted her back to the office.

All the long, windy afternoon, the letter lay unopened on Polly's desk. Already everyone in the office knew about it and the corridors buzzed with gossip. Lord Peter must have been interested in Polly after all to write to her on the day his engagement was announced. Sir Edward heard of it through the office grapevine and harrumphed all the way to his club. Mr. Baines, who had grown very fond of Polly as the days of his bachelordom lengthened, secretly hoped that it was not bad news. He secretly felt that Lord Peter was a shallow sort of chap.

All the long walk back to the hostel, Polly was aware of the letter in her reticule. She waited until she had shut and locked the door of her room and removed her hat, stabbing the long hatpins into the pincushion as if it were Lord Peter's fickle heart.

Then gingerly picking up the letter as if it were a live bomb, she opened it and read:

*My Dearest Polly,*

*By the time you read this you will probably have read all that nonsense about my engagement in* The Times. *Please pay no attention. My darling, there is no way anything can stop us having a happy future together. I shall be arriving home in time for the office party and I shall tell you of my plans. It will mean you will have to leave Westerman's, my poor slave, but I'm sure you will enjoy being a lady of leisure. We belong together, Polly. My sweet girl, I can hardly wait to hold you in my arms again.*

*Yours only,*
*Peter*

117

Polly jumped to her feet and twirled around the room. He meant to marry her. He said so! Nature seemed to celebrate as well, for the wind outside died as suddenly as it had sprung up and a thin, pale, weak sunlight gilded the sooty roofs and a starling imitated a blackbird in Gordon Square around the corner, bringing with its song a false illusion of spring.

*     *     *

Now the Marquis of Wollerton should have been a very happy man. It is not, after all, every day that one is proved so triumphantly right. He could not, therefore, understand why he was so depressed.

He had been so low in spirits that when Angela, Lady Bansbury, had telephoned to remind him that he was expected to grace her musicale that evening, all his well-thought-out excuses had fled and he had promised to attend.

Now, he was fidgeting on a little gilt chair and dismally waiting for some stout German to finally come to the end of a long, long repertoire of lieder. At last when he thought he would have to scream aloud, the singer hit the last sonorous note and the marquis was free to rise and make his escape.

He was working his way toward the doorway when he was accosted by a very fashionably dressed middle-aged lady. It took him a few seconds to recognize a singularly rejuvenated Lady Blenkinsop. He complimented her on her appearance and she blushed prettily. 'Everyone should get rid of their spouse at some time,' she beamed. 'Of course your mother was quite furious with me because I did not put Miss Marsh in her place, but really it's all for the best. I mean, Peter *is* engaged to someone else.'

'My mother ... Peter ... I don't understand,' said the marquis.

'Come with me and we'll hide behind those desiccated palms,' said Lady Blenkinsop.

'Well!' she remarked when they were seated. 'You must not tell your mother ...' She then told him of her visit from the duchess.

'My mother has gone too far this time,' said the marquis angrily. 'How dare she poke her nose into my affairs.'

'But it wasn't *your* affairs,' said Lady Blenkinsop slyly. 'Peter's affairs, surely.'

'Nonetheless,' said the marquis stiffly, 'I feel that Miss Marsh has been badly treated. One of us should call on her and—'

'And who better than yourself,' interrupted Lady Blenkinsop sweetly.

'You don't expect my mother to go,' said the marquis, getting to his feet. 'I shall see if I can persuade that dragon who guards the hostel to let me see her.'

'Tell Miss Marsh to call on me,' said Lady Blenkinsop, also getting to her feet. 'I am deeply indebted to her.'

'You are a heartless woman,' laughed the marquis. 'Are you never going to see poor Sir Edward again?'

She sighed. 'I suppose I must. But not just for the moment. I am having *such* fun.'

★     ★     ★

The hostel in Euston was in darkness by the time the marquis arrived. He realized uncomfortably that he should go away but he was overcome by a sudden desire to see Polly and comfort her. He manfully pressed the bell.

After a few minutes a disembodied white

face stared at him through the glass and then the door was cautiously opened an inch to reveal Miss Thistlethwaite with a massive wrapper clutched to her throat and her hair bristling with curl papers.

'My lord,' she gasped, recognizing her aristocratic visitor from the society photographs in *The Tatler*. 'It is *eleven o'clock*.'

'I have come to see Miss Marsh on an urgent matter,' said the marquis in his most aristocratic tone.

Miss Thistlethwaite was torn between curiosity and her natural desire to exert her authority. Curiosity won. Holding open the door, she ushered him past the pampas grass and into the gloom of the sitting room, where the high-backed, hard upright chairs stood in their unwelcoming group. Miss Thistlethwaite lit the gas and bustled importantly up the stairs.

Polly climbed up through layers of dreams and staggered, half awake, to answer the persistent knocking at the door. Miss Thistlethwaite's fat face swimming in the darkness of the corridor looked for a moment like the extension of her dreams. But then the all-too-real fruity accents informed her that 'one of her aristocratic friends' was awaiting her in the sitting room. Polly lit her candle feverishly—the use of gas was not encouraged during the night hours—and then scrambled into her clothes. It must be Peter. Dear, dear Peter! Who else could it be?

Miss Thistlethwaite was entertaining the marquis with tepid tea and tepid conversation when Polly erupted into the sitting room and stood frozen with dismay at the sight of the marquis's face. 'I thought you were . . .' she began, but the marquis held up a long, white-gloved hand to silence her.

'Thank you for your hospitality, Miss Thistlethwaite, and now, if you will excuse us . . .'

Miss Thistlethwaite rose reluctantly to her feet and seemed to take hours to leave the room. By the time the door was closed Polly had recovered her composure. Her future brother-in-law had no doubt hastened to make a social call. He looked very remote and aloof in his impeccable evening dress. Polly sat down primly on one of the hard chairs and smiled at him inquiringly. The marquis groaned to himself. Obviously she had not read *The Times*.

122

'Miss Marsh,' he began in his attractive husky voice, 'I do not know whether you have seen the announcement of Peter's engagement—'

'Oh, *yes*,' interrupted Polly blithely. 'But that is all a lot of nonsense. I confess, all the same, that I was very upset until I received Peter's letter of explanation.'

'There can be no explanation, dear girl, other than the obvious one, that Peter is engaged to Miss Bryant-Pettigrew.'

'Peter states quite clearly that he wishes to marry me,' said Polly firmly, radiant with beauty and confidence.

'Nonsense!' The chilly denial echoed around the wavering shadows of the room.

'I shall show you the letter. Wait there!' Polly jumped to her feet and rushed from the room. She was soon back, brandishing the letter like a flag.

The marquis took it silently and opened the stiff pages. As he read his brother's letter, he was prey to a series of strange emotions. His first reaction was one of relief, the second anger, and the third, cold and fastidious distaste. His hooded lids covering the expression of his pale-gold eyes, he placed the letter on the table and said quietly, 'He says nothing of marriage.'

'Not in so many words,' retorted Polly, looking amused. 'What a difficult man you are to convince! One would think that the Marquis of Wollerton did not want Polly Marsh as a sister-in-law.'

'I don't,' he remarked. 'I think you might be too good for my brother. I don't want to hurt you. Can't you *see* that? But if you go on believing that Peter is going to marry you, you are going to be even more hurt in the end. It's as plain as day that he is telling you that his engagement and marriage will not affect your future position as . . . his mistress.'

She got to her feet and stood looking down at him with quaint dignity. 'You do not think much of me after all, my lord,' she said. 'I would not have let Peter hold me and kiss me if I had not been sure that his intentions were honorable.'

The marquis felt his temper rising. He did not know that Peter's 'holding and kissing' of Polly was one very chaste occasion in St. James's Park, and so a series of lurid and tantalizing pictures flashed through his mind with all the jerky rapidity of the latest bioscope show.

'*I* held you and kissed you,' he said in a low voice.

Polly turned her back to him. 'That was none of my doing,' she said in a suffocated voice. 'Please leave, my lord.'

He stood, irresolute, looking at the slim back facing him and at the faint blue veins on the slender neck topped with its golden mass of curls.

He slowly put his arms around her and held her to him. 'But you responded, my Polly,' he said huskily and he bent his head and kissed the back of her neck.

Polly stood very still. The hot lips seemed to burn her skin and the man's overwhelming virility made her knees tremble. She had a sudden languorous longing to turn and put her arms around his neck. Instead she said in a chilly little voice, 'I see, my lord, that you are confusing your own intentions with those of your brother. I will marry Peter with or without his family's approval. Good evening.'

She walked quickly from the room, leaving him standing there feeling a strange mixture of anger and pain.

*        *        *

Polly did not reply to Peter's letter. It was marvelous to think that he would be sailing

125

for home before any reply of hers could reach him. But most of the pleasure of anticipation had gone. Every time she tried to conjure up his face, it was the marquis's face that looked down at her, it was the marquis's lips she felt. As the morning at Westerman's wore on, her typing became more erratic. She had typed 'Peaking, Pekking, Pekign' five times and torn up five letters before she had achieved the simple address of the office in Peking. She had arrived at the office that morning at the same time as Amy Feathers and Bob Friend. Bob had looked at Polly with his eyes glowing and Amy had looked at Bob. *Why, she's in love with him*, thought Polly, wondering how on earth she had not noticed it before. She had given Amy a warm and sympathetic smile and received a cold stare in return for her pains.

Now all Polly wanted to do was to rush to Shoreditch and pour out the whole story to her mother. But she had a sneaking feeling that her mother would agree with the marquis. That letter! After the marquis had left the evening before, she had read and reread it until her eyes ached.

Some of the times it had looked like a pure and touching declaration of innocent love; at others, it seemed like a sleazy outburst of lust. If *only* she could remember Peter properly as she had known him. But every memory was soiled by the picture of the sneering marquis and the memory of his lips against her skin.

It was almost lunchtime when Mr. Baines ushered Lady Blenkinsop into her small office. Her ladyship was attired from throat to ankle in magnificent Russian sable, her face was delicately rouged, and a saucy little feather hat was perched on her newly curled hair.

'I shall tell your husband you are here,' said Mr. Baines with a deferential bow.

Lady Blenkinsop waved her hand. 'No, please don't. Are you by any chance, Mister Baines, the office manager?'

'I have that honor, my lady,' said Mr. Baines, desperately wishing that he had had time to remove his cardboard shirt-sleeve protectors and don his jacket. His braces were of a bright, lurid red and embroidered with small Scottie dogs—his one outward concession to dashing bachelor freedom—and he hoped Lady Blenkinsop would not find him frivolous because of it.

'Ah, Mister Baines. I have heard of you,' said Lady Blenkinsop, taking out a small lace handkerchief and releasing a gentle aroma of Fleurs d'Antan around the stuffy office. 'I was just about to ask Miss Marsh to join me for lunch. Perhaps you would care to come as well, Mister Baines?'

'G-gratified! Hon-honored!' gabbled Mr. Baines, running a finger along the inside of his celluloid collar.

'Good! That's settled,' said Lady Blenkinsop airily. 'We will go to your usual luncheon place. It will be divine to see the City gentlemen at play.'

She swept regally from the office, not looking around to see if they were following her. Polly and Mr. Baines trotted breathlessly after her, pulling on their coats.

Mr. Baines was dimly aware of the astonished admiration of his friends at Spielmann's. The menu swam before his eyes and he automatically ordered the same as Lady Blenkinsop, as did Polly.

Polly desperately wondered why Lady Blenkinsop had called on her but she was never to know. Lady Blenkinsop turned the full battery of her attention on the bemused office manager and bombarded him with questions. Since these were all about his work and since Lady Blenkinsop had insisted on ordering wine with the meal, Mr. Baines slowly began to relax. The aura of admiration emanating from his friends acted upon his senses more than the wine. He felt himself sparkling as he had never done before. Hoary office jokes were treated by Lady Blenkinsop as the height of wit and her tinkling laughter rang out over the hum of conversation in the chophouse.

Polly began to glance nervously at the watch pinned to her bosom. Lady Blenkinsop was talking of the enchantment of Venice and the glory of Paris and Mr. Baines was sitting drinking it all in, his middle-aged features the happy ghost of the young and carefree man he used to be. At last Polly found a break in their conversation and reminded them of the time. Both looked surprised to see she was still there.

'Run along, my dear,' said Lady Blenkinsop. 'I shall just sit here a little longer and talk to dear Mister Baines. I am sure Westerman's can spare him for a little longer.'

Mr. Baines banished the thought of the piles of work waiting for him as Lady Blenkinsop said good-bye to Polly. 'Do telephone me as soon as ever you can,' said

Lady Blenkinsop, 'and we'll have such *long* chats.'

They had resumed their conversation before Polly had left the table.

The long City afternoon wore on and still Mr. Albert Baines did not return, but Joe Noakes, one of the messengers, told Amy who told Bob Friend who told Polly, that Mr. Baines had been seen departing in Lady Blenkinsop's carriage and that, as the staid office manager had helped her ladyship into her carriage, he had *squeezed her hand*. Work at Westerman's had ceased while this delicious piece of gossip was mulled over. Why didn't Polly join them?

But the haughty Miss Marsh merely replied that she *never* gossiped about her *friends* and the much subdued Mr. Friend took that flea in his ear back to the more congenial company of Amy Feathers.

## CHAPTER EIGHT

The office party was to be held two days before Christmas. On her latest visit to Stone Lane, Polly had found to her embarrassment that she was meant to spend

130

Christmas at home. Now Polly fully expected to be spending Christmas with the Duke and Duchess of Westerman and was at long last faced with the necessity of telling Mrs. Marsh of her hopes and ambitions.

Mrs. Marsh had held out one pudgy, work-reddened hand for the precious letter. She popped a pair of steel-rimmed glasses on the end of her nose and sat down heavily at the kitchen table to give the matter her full attention. Joyce and baby Alf were asleep, Alf senior was in the pub, and Gran had gone with him to imbibe her weekly glass of port and lemon.

Her lips moving slightly, Mrs. Marsh carefully read from beginning to end and then dropped the letter on the table and wiped her hands carefully on her apron.

'You're a fool, Pol,' she said heavily. 'Yerse. A silly, little, snobby fool. That there Lord Peter ain't got marriage in mind. 'E wants up your skirts, my girl.'

Polly blushed at her mother's coarseness and became more determined than ever to escape from the working-class mud of Stone Lane. Her love for her mother vanished in a wave of fury.

'All everyone ever does is to try to keep

me down,' she said icily. 'I am leaving now, Mother, and I shall not return until I am Lady Burley. You will be sorry for your lack of trust.'

The small figure of Mrs. Marsh suddenly seemed formidable in the small kitchen. 'Take yerself off, then, me girl,' she said slowly, 'and finds it out for ye'self the 'ard way. God will punish yer for yer snotty ways, see if 'e don't.'

'Good day to you,' said Polly with awful hauteur.

'Ah, garn ... yer bleedin' little fool,' said Mrs. Marsh heavily. She moved to the fire and began to poke it heartily, keeping her back to her daughter, and listening to the angry rap of Polly's heels as she descended the stairs and slammed the street door behind her.

Mrs. Marsh wiped away the angry tears from her eyes and lumbered over to the sideboard and extracted a few precious sheets of writing paper and a bottle of ink and a steel pen.

Sitting down at the kitchen table again, she bent her head over the paper and slowly and painfully began to write, 'The Most Honorable Marquis of Wollerton, My Lord Marquis...'

The large conference room at Westerman's had been set aside for the party. Staff were to be allowed one hour and a half to go home and change for the great event. The Duke of Westerman was not expected to attend, much to Polly's disappointment, but she never doubted for a minute that Peter would be there. She had read in the social columns that his boat had docked at Southampton the day before. There had been no mention of any Miss Bryant-Pettigrew—not that she had expected any, Polly told herself firmly.

One of Lady Jellings' evening gowns was pressed and ready in the small room in the hostel. Polly now lifted it over her head, shivering slightly as the cool silk touched her skin. It was of a deep kingfisher-blue, cut daringly low on the bosom and opened down the front to reveal an underdress of snowy flounces of lace. Polly's small looking glass told her that she had never looked more beautiful but in her heart she felt ugly. The Christmas presents for her family lay wrapped under the bed but she had not had the courage to return to Stone

Lane and face her mother's angry disdain.

She thought wistfully of the cosy flat in Stone Lane. The kitchen would be redolent of all the smells of Christmas—plum pudding, turkey, brandy, hot chestnuts, tangerines, and the tangy smell of pine from the tree—and little Alf's face would be shining as he sat by the fire and tried to stay awake to see Santa Claus. Every rattling loose slate on the roof would be the sound of a tiny hoof, every drunken laugh from the pub at the corner, the jolly laugh of the Christmas saint. Her ambition had removed her from it all and she felt immeasurably young and vulnerable as she collected her stole and fan and hurried out into the wintry street to look for a cab.

A light snow had been falling for the past hour and as Polly clattered into the City the tall buildings were etched with white and the cobbled streets were silent and deserted. A chill feeling of dread clutched at her heart and she wondered for the first time whether Peter Burley would come.

★　　　★　　　★

The duchess put down her planchette after unsuccessfully trying to raise the spirits of the dead and stared in open dismay at her elder son.

'Westerman's party? But Peter said nothing of it to me! We have all sorts of people coming to dinner including some of the Bryant-Pettigrews' relatives. He *can't* go.'

'He already has,' said the marquis grimly, crumpling Mrs. Marsh's letter in his hand.

'Well, don't just *stand* there, Edward. Go and fetch him back.'

'Peter is not a child, Mother, and he does work for Westerman's. There is nothing I can do about it.'

'I know it's that Marsh girl. I just know it,' wailed the duchess. 'Edward, *please*. Peter has been doing so well and not a breath of scandal must reach the ears of the Bryant-Pettigrews. As I told you, their relatives will be here tonight and they're due here next week!'

'It is Peter's affair, not mine,' said the marquis testily. How do mothers expect their children to grow up if . . .' He broke off as he remembered the pathetic plea from Mrs. Marsh in his hand and sighed heavily. 'All right, Mother. I'll go and bring him back.'

Despite the speed of his new Sunbeam Mabley motorcar, the thickening snow finally reduced him to a crawl. By the time he had changed motorcar for carriage at his town house—not trusting modern transport to cope with winter conditions—he estimated Westerman's party must have started an hour ago.

Perhaps Peter would not be there after all.

*　　*　　*

Lady Blenkinsop yawned and stretched like a cat and slowly opened her eyes. For a minute, she could not remember where she was as her sleepy eyes roamed over the small overly-furnished bedroom. Then they came to rest affectionately on the knobby bones of Mr. Baines's back as he turned up the gas.

'You look funny naked,' she giggled. 'You still look as if you've got a sort of bumpy white City suit on.'

Albert Baines blushed. He could feel the blush rising from his hammertoes to the top of his bald spot and hurriedly put on his long woollen combinations. He could never become accustomed to Jennie Blenkinsop's lack of inhibitions, unaware that Lady Blenkinsop was quite amazed at it herself.

'I must go to the office party,' he said, carefully averting his eyes from her small naked bosom that was emerging from beneath the covers.

'Can I come too?' she asked lazily.

Mr. Baines looked startled. 'But Sir Edward is bound to be there . . .'

'So?'

'So—I will be terribly embarrassed and probably lose my job,' he said with some vigor.

'No you won't, my darling office slave. And anyway, I've got lots of money. Why don't we run away together to somewhere splendid?'

Albert struggled into his boiled shirt. 'Because I would feel strange, Jennie. I've been a working man all my life. I'm not used to your world.'

'It's much the same as yours,' said Lady Blenkinsop. 'Anyway, I'm coming to your party. I want to gossip to the beautiful Miss Marsh. You must help me dress, you know. I could not possibly bring my maid, although this haven of Hampstead respectability would no doubt appeal to her.'

Mr. Baines looked at her with baffled adoration. He would never understand her. He would never stop loving her.

When they were finally dressed, they descended the oaken stairs. Albert suddenly stopped and wrapped his long, bony arms about her and held her close. 'You won't let anything happen to spoil this, Jennie?' he said. 'I suddenly feel afraid.'

'My poor Bertie,' she said, kissing him affectionately. 'Always the worrier. Now what could happen on this beautiful Christmas?'

As if in answer, the doorbell clanged. The small parlormaid ran to answer it. Mr. Baines opened his mouth to tell her not to but no sound came out. The door swung open, and a cloud of snow swirled in from the Heath and settled on the shiny parquet of the hall floor. Gladys Baines and Sir Edward Blenkinsop stood on the doorstep.

The Baines's cook had written to inform her mistress of 'the dreadful goings-on' and Gladys had immediately enlisted the aid of Sir Edward.

There was a long silence while both couples confronted each other. Then Mrs. Baines began to sob. The large, domineering women was softened by her vulnerability and tears, reminding Bertie of the young, slim girl he had married so long ago when the world was young and the Heath stretched all the way to Samarkand.

Sir Edward looked like a whipped dog, his bloodshot eyes turned pathetically up toward his wife. Lady Blenkinsop could feel her vitality draining away bit by bit. Her voice reached Bertie's ears, the sad ghost of a whisper: 'Our dreams are over. The time has come for us to go home.'

She moved down the stairs like an old woman and took her husband's arm and went out with him into the snow without looking back.

Bertie Baines reflected that hearts did not break; nothing so physical happened. A piece of the soul had been torn out from him leaving a great gaping wound which would never heal. He looked down at his wife. 'Come, Gladys,' he said gently. 'If you hurry and change, I can take you to the office party. Come, come,' he added, moving slowly toward her. Dry your eyes, that's my girl. There, there. We'll talk about it all later. But not now. Please God, not now.'

The conference room managed to look grim and foreboding despite the gaudy paper decorations. Some optimistic soul had hung a large bunch of mistletoe on the chandelier but no one looked in danger of kissing each other—or even of speaking to each other. In the hope that the duke would grace it with his presence, the organization of the party had been allocated to Sir Edward who, on hearing of the duke's refusal to attend, had done very little about it.

Not only had Sir Edward failed to put in an appearance, but he had provided nothing in the way of drink. The best crystal glasses were lined up at the end of the conference table but there was nothing to put in them. After the first quarter of an hour had passed in whispers and the chill of the musty room began to creep into the very bones of the guests, Mr. and Mrs. Baines arrived exuding all the jollity of a wake.

The directors clustered eagerly around Mr. Baines. What should they do? Damned fellow Blenkinsop had done absolutely nothing!

Mr. Baines gave a wild distracted look

140

around the room while his subdued wife clutched his arm like an amorous gorilla. 'The directors' champagne,' he said. 'Six crates were delivered just yesterday. You know, sirs, the stuff we keep for visitors.'

Splendid chap! Saved the day. The beautiful green bottles appeared as if by magic. Pop! Pop! Pop! And the directors' wives started to talk to each other. More pops and the directors' wives talked to the clerks' wives. Still more pops and the directors' wives complimented young Amy Feathers on her gown. She had made it herself! How cunning!

Polly stood ignored at the edge of the room. The directors' wives had not forgotten the picnic. The girl was much too pushing, and the directors themselves did not want to talk to someone who was on familiar terms with the Westermans. The clerks were tired of Polly's hoity-toity ways, and even Bob Friend felt that he had been snubbed once too often.

Polly tried hard not to mind. When Peter arrived they would all find that she was far above them.

The door swung open and Lord Peter Burley breezed in. He was warmly greeted and slapped on the back by the directors.

He drank several glasses of champagne. He talked to Mr. Baines and drank several more. He flirted with the delighted clerks' wives and drank many more. He glanced at the mistletoe and insisted on kissing Amy Feathers to roars of applause from the now well-lubricated party. Would he never notice her? He moved off into a corner with Mr. Baines and sat down, and soon the two men were deep in conversation.

Then he looked across the room and saw Polly and winked.

A small, cold hand of misgiving clutched at Polly's stomach. There had been nothing loverlike in that wink. He was coming toward her; he was smiling. She gazed up into his glinting green eyes and wondered how she could have ever forgotten what he looked like.

'Darling Polly,' he said in a thick voice. 'Bainsey-boy has told me of a splendid place where we can be alone.'

Polly was aware of Mr. Baines staring at her worriedly from across the room. 'Come *now*,' whispered Peter. 'Nobody's looking.' He opened the door and pulled her outside into the corridor. Polly felt suddenly breathless and lighthearted. Everything was going to be all right.

Peter led the way to a showroom at the back of the office building and threw open the door. It was used to display all the splendors of the east to visiting buyers. Ivory, jade, and brass shone in the light, buddhas from China, many-armed goddesses from India, silks from Japan, peacocks' feathers from Kashmir, tusks from Africa, coral from the West Indies, and piles and piles of Oriental rugs. Peter drew the unresisting Polly down onto a pile of these and took her hands in his. The moment had come.

She turned her head shyly away and stared at a small bearded peasant who endlessly poled his ivory boat across a sea of jade.

Then strong hands were forcing her head around and hot lips still wet with champagne were pressed against her own. She surrendered herself to his kiss wondering why nothing was happening to her senses. At last she drew gently away.

'Peter—you said you would discuss our future.'

'Later, darling,' he murmured impatiently, his lips against her hair. 'I've waited so long.'

Polly once again let herself be drawn into

his embrace. But where was the cool, dashing, young aristocrat she remembered? His face was flushed and his breathing ragged. His hands seemed to be everywhere, probing and stroking. He murmured endearments in a thick voice, as if they were obscenities. She felt a draft of cold air on her legs and realized, with horror, that he had lifted her skirt and one determined hand was crawling up the inside of her leg.

She jerked away and pulled her skirts down only to find that the other roving hand had slid down the front of her dress and was clasping her bosom. Terrified images flashed through her brain. "*E only wants up yer skirts, my girl,*' said the voice of Mrs. Marsh. Then she seemed to be looking up at the painted ceiling of Bevington Chase, where the man with the horns and goats' feet perpetually clutched a large white breast in one tanned and horny hand.

'Peter!' she wailed, pushing him away with all her strength. 'Can't you wait until we are married?'

Lord Peter's clutching hands went suddenly still and he sat bolt upright. His champagne-glazed green eyes focussed on

144

the flushed and furious Polly.

'Married!' he hooted. 'Whatever gave you the idea that I would marry *you*. Good heavens, I'm engaged to a perfectly suitable girl, but that need not interfere with *our* future together. Come, Polly. You were *made* for fun.'

Polly's dream world whirled and crashed. She got slowly to her feet, smoothing down her dress with trembling fingers, and backed away from him toward the door. 'I thought you loved me,' she whispered.

'Of *course* I do,' he answered in an exasperated voice. 'But you must see that marriage with one of your sort is strictly out of the question.'

Gone was the dream Polly, the debutante Polly, the gracious Lady Polly. Miss Marsh of Stone Lane raised her small hand and struck Lord Peter as hard as she could, right across his face, and then turned and opened the door.

The next minute, she was wrenched back and thrown down on top of the pile of rugs again and Lord Peter dived on top of her.

'You little hellcat! You'll pay for that, my darling guttersnipe. I know your type. You led me on and now you're going to pay the penalty.' He forced his mouth down on hers. One minute Polly was struggling and biting and kicking—and the next she found herself looking up at Lord Peter, who seemed to be floating in midair.

The Marquis of Wollerton, who had picked his little brother up by the seat of the pants and the scruff of the neck, hurled him across the room. 'Get out of here,' snapped the marquis to Polly. 'Go back to the party and act as if nothing has happened. Do not leave without me.'

Polly fled. She blundered sightlessly along the corridors toward the noise of the party and then stopped and leaned her hot head against the cold wall. Waves of shame engulfed her. This is what came of despising her fellow workers and being ashamed of her family.

In her attempts to enlarge her education at the theater, Polly had attended a production of Mr. George Bernard Shaw's *Man and Superman* at the Criterion. Now a passage from the play rang in her ears: '*We live in an atmosphere of shame. We are ashamed of everything that is real about us; ashamed of ourselves, of our relatives, of our incomes, of our accents, of our opinions, of our experience, just as we are ashamed of our naked skins.*'

She edged into the room but nobody seemed to notice her. She stood on the outside of a happy office world to which she could have so easily belonged. Amy was surrounded by a small court of admirers. Her thin face was flushed and her eyes were like stars. Now jealousy was added to Polly's other burning emotions of anger and shame. She wanted to kill Lord Peter, she wanted to kill herself, she wanted to run away—all at the same moment.

The door behind her opened and the marquis came in alone. She watched him with dull eyes as he moved about the room, shaking hands with the staff, saying a pleasant word here and there. How he must despise her!

At last he came toward her, accompanied by Mr. Baines.

'Mister Baines was just agreeing with me that you should not go home at this time of night unescorted. The wives have their husbands and Mister Friend is accompanying Miss Feathers. I have suggested to Mister Baines that it would be a good idea if I saw you safely to your doorstep. Is that not so, Mister Baines?'

'Quite,' said Mr. Baines in a dull, flat

voice.

'And as it is snowing quite heavily, I suggest we leave now.'

Polly bowed her head in assent and took his offered arm. Now everyone was watching her—Miss Marsh leaving with a marquis. Polly would rather have had the comforting escort of Bob Friend.

They climbed into the carriage in silence and in silence moved through the glittering white streets of the City. The snow had ceased to fall. Down Ludgate Hill the carriage trotted as its occupants sat in either corner, each wrapped in their miserable thoughts. *'If that is love,'* Polly was thinking, *'all that heavy breathing and panting and fumbling, I want nothing to do with it.'*

The marquis was feeling that he ought to make some apology on behalf of his family, yet did not know quite how to begin. The thick snow muffled the horses' hooves as the carriage rolled silently along the Strand. The raucous cries of the merrymakers under the flaring gaslights and all the particular smells of the Strand—cigars and patchouli mixed with beer and roasting chestnuts—seemed a world away.

By the time they reached Euston the soot

from London's thousands of chimneys was already speckling the snow with black.

The marquis was becoming alarmed at the intensity of his feelings. Polly Marsh had surely received no more than she deserved. But he had an overwhelming longing to take her in his arms and kiss away the hurt. He wanted to protect her. He wanted to marry her!

He was so amazed at the insanity of the idea that it took him a few minutes to realize that Polly was trying to say good-bye.

'Polly,' he said gently, unaware that he was using her first name. 'Wouldn't it be better to go home?'

'Home? I *am* home,' said Polly, waving her fan toward the hostel.

'I mean Stone Lane. If you would like to collect your belongings, I can take you there.'

Polly wanted to escape from his company. But she also longed for home. 'All right,' she said hurriedly. 'I'll be very quick.'

She sprang lightly from the carriage and ran into the hostel.

In a surprisingly short time she reappeared carrying a small trunk and a shopping bag full of Christmas parcels that she shyly handed to the footman.

The carriage jerked forward and the two occupants sat in silence again.

At last the marquis said quietly, 'Talk about it, Polly. Talk about Peter. Don't keep it all inside.'

She shook her head dumbly and he could see the glint of tears in the corner of her eyes.

'You are not the only one who has these humiliating experiences. Shall I tell you about mine?' He went on without waiting for her reply.

'I was just seventeen and had finished my studies at Eton. One of my best friends was a youth called Gerald Parkenshaw. He had a twin sister called Penelope and all us boys adored her. She was tiny, elfin, with masses of glossy black curls. We teased her and called her Madcap Penny but we were all secretly in love with her.

'Well, the twins' parents were giving an end-of-term party and all Gerald's Etonian friends were invited, including me. I knew the other boys had all planned to bring Penny silly, funny gifts, like stuffed animals or love poems, but I decided to steal a march on them and be grown-up and different. My parents were ridiculously generous about my allowance and I had saved up enough to buy a small diamond ring. I was going to lure Penny into the conservatory at the party, present the ring, and declare my love on bended knee. All this I told to brother Gerald.

'The big night arrived. Penny was all in white and had never looked more lovely. When it came my turn to dance with her, I was trembling with nerves but, plucking up my courage, I suggested that the ballroom was too stuffy and that it would be a jolly idea to stroll in the conservatory. She said, "What fun!" and led the way with singularly unmaidenly enthusiasm. Undeterred however, I sank to one knee and seized her hand. I told her all sorts of rot. I said she was a goddess and that I was only fit to kiss the hem of her gown—which I did. I then begged her to be my wife. I rose to my feet and presented her with the tiny diamond ring. And what did my love say? She said, "Oh, you *silly* chump, Eddie!" and burst into peals of laughter. And out from behind the palms came all my old school chums, laughing fit to burst.

'I felt I would die with shame and humiliation. I felt the whole world was staring at me and jeering. But next day everyone had forgotten about it—except of course Gerald, because I took him aside and punched his head for telling his sister about my plans.

'I saw Penny only last week. She has turned into a fat, bullying woman with a strident voice and her husband—she married a merchant banker—spends as much time abroad as he possibly can.

'To end this long story—I think Peter will grow into a very pompous businessman.'

'But you did not cause the humiliation by pretending to be someone other than yourself,' said Polly slowly. 'You were not social climbing.'

'No,' he replied equally gently. 'But I did rather fancy myself as the great lover. Were you in love with Peter?'

Polly shook her head. 'I thought it would be so marvelous to be "my lady." I was in love with that. I am as much to blame as Peter. I shall never try to step out of my class again.'

'Come!' cried the marquis, feeling slightly alarmed at such penitence. 'Don't go rushing off in the other direction and marry a costermonger. Just be yourself,

Polly Marsh, and nothing very bad will happen to you.'

'I'll try,' she said simply. 'I left all Lady Jellings' gowns with Miss Thistlethwaite. I don't want to wear castoffs again.'

'Must you always go to extremes?' said the marquis crossly. 'They were perfectly charming frocks.'

'Oh!' snapped Polly. 'You don't know what you're talking about. It's easy for you. You are at the top of the social tree and everyone toadies to you.'

'Except Polly Marsh,' he said, smiling faintly.

The carriage had come to a halt.

'This is good-bye, my lord,' said Polly, holding out her hand.

'Shall we not see each other again?'

'I don't think so, my lord,' said Polly, with her hand on the strap.

'Then kiss me good-bye, Polly Marsh,' he teased.

She leaned forward and kissed him quickly on his thin cheek but he gently drew her to him and bent his mouth to hers. Her whole body seemed to melt into that one kiss. They finally drew apart, breathless and shaken.

'Come with me, Polly. Stay with me,'

said the marquis huskily.

She recoiled from him with her gloved hand to her mouth. 'Oh!' she cried piteously. 'You are every bit as bad as your brother.'

'I didn't mean . . . I meant . . .' he cried, stretching his hand forward. But the carriage door slammed and his footman was already on the pavement to help Polly with her bags.

He must explain himself. He made a move as if to leave the carriage and sank back with a groan. What *had* he meant? To marry her? Nonsense. He had only meant . . . Oh, what did it all matter. The girl was very beautiful and the directors' champagne had been very heady. He would come to his senses in the morning.

Polly felt that this evening of seesawing emotions would never end. She pushed open the kitchen door and braced herself to meet her mother.

Mrs. Marsh turned from the kitchen range and surveyed her daughter. 'Don't jest stand there, Pol,' she said finally. 'Take yer things upstairs. I saved yer a bit of supper. Thought yer might be comin' 'ome.' The rest of the family looked at Polly silently.

'Ma!' said Polly, her voice breaking. 'Oh, *Ma.*'

'There, there, ducks,' crooned her mother, moving with surprising speed. She hustled Polly from the kitchen and up the stairs to her old, familiar room.

'Naow, then,' said Mrs. Marsh, settling herself comfortably in an armchair. 'You just go ahead and 'ave a good cry and then you tell your Ma all about it.'

The rest of the family sat in the kitchen listening to the sounds of broken sobbing from above and then the murmur of quiet voices. Not even Alf Marsh considered going to investigate. Mrs. Marsh was ruler of her small kingdom and all laws and decisions were made by her.

\*     \*     \*

Mr. Baines lay beside his sleeping wife and stared up into the darkness of their bedroom ceiling and felt that his world had come to an end. Had he been a more callous man—yes, might as well admit it, a less *decent* man—he would have told Gladys to take her shrill voice and bullying ways straight back to her mother. But the new Edwardian liberalism had not penetrated to his Victorian soul. So he had done the 'right thing.' Why then, did he feel so terrible?

Had he not felt so terrible, he would never have told Lord Peter to take Polly to the deserted stockroom.

An elusive aroma of Fleurs d'Antan still lingered in the chilly bedroom, like a memory of a golden summer. Mr. Albert Baines clenched his teeth to stop a groan from escaping and buried his aching head in his pillow.

★　　　★　　　★

'Hah!' said Sir Edward Blenkinsop loudly. 'Harrumph!' But the sleeping figure of his wife did not move. He stood in his long nightshirt glaring at the motionless woman lying on the bed. Her face looked drawn and old even in repose, and it made him feel obscurely guilty. But a wife's place was with her husband, by Jove. He had done the right thing, hadn't he? He'd forgiven her, hadn't he?

He had expected her to fall into his arms out of sheer gratitude. But she had complained of a headache and taken a large dose of laudanum and promptly gone to bed. It struck him that ever since their wedding night he had rarely seen his wife awake. Once again she had fled from him into some country of dreams where he could not follow. He thought of that cosy little armful he had tucked away in a flat in the King's Road. Dammit! It was different for men. Wasn't it?

*     *     *

Amy Feathers clasped her thin knees to her chest and stared out at the falling snow. It was all so hopeless. Bob Friend had taken her home. He had held her in his arms right on her own doorstep. He had kissed her and it had been the most wonderful, magical thing that had ever, ever happened to her. Then he had buried his lips in her hair and whispered, 'Polly!'

The Salvation Army carol singers were trumpeting out 'God Rest Ye Merry Gentlemen' at the corner of the street. It rang in Amy's ears like a dirge.

*     *     *

Lord Peter arrived late to his parents' house party and despite his battered appearance— he had been set upon by a gang of thugs he had explained—set himself to please. The Bryant-Pettigrew relatives were delighted with him. What a splendid, upright young man. The very backbone of England. The very flower of English manhood. Splendid chap!

It was going to be a jolly Christmas after all, thought Peter. He had quite put that embarrassing and squalid little incident with that office girl out of his head. One of the new chambermaids had looked at him just that evening with a very roguish twinkle in her eye. The world was full of delightful women just waiting for the charms of Peter Burley.

He put a sprig of mistletoe in his buttonhole in case he should bump into the pretty chambermaid on the road to bed.

★　　★　　★

The Marquis of Wollerton went to his club and got well and truly drunk for the first time in his life.

# CHAPTER NINE

Christmas and Boxing Day crept past under leaden skies. The year was dead. The sparrows seemed to mourn as they hunched their little bodies on the warmth of sooty windowsills, and the starlings serenaded the dark sky with their long, descending metallic notes.

All too soon the working day dawned for Polly. She had told her mother that she never wanted to see Westerman's again. Mrs. Marsh had been horrified. One third of the country was living on starvation level. Unemployment was worse than during Victorian times. To turn down a good job was downright unchristian. She should be thankful that the only punishment her Maker had seen fit to mete out was a certain amount of social embarrassment. Mrs. Marsh bitterly regretted the elocution lessons. She deserved to be punished herself for giving her daughter ideas above her station. Polly must never, ever forget again that she was the daughter of working-class parents. A marriage into the lower middle class was possible, but no higher.

Polly certainly thought she would never forget her position in life again. Never again did she want to see the Westermans or listen to their lazy, condescending drawls or face their hard, arrogant eyes.

But as she walked down the Kingsland Road toward the City, she did experience a twinge of regret over having given away all those beautiful clothes.

What Dickens would call 'a London particular' had descended on the metropolis. Thick, suffocating, yellow fog blanketed the streets and alleys. Dressed once more in her office serge, Polly reflected that her frock would be filthy enough for the scrap heap by the time she finished work that day.

The gaslights were still burning in the shop windows, small islands of warmth in a city of dreadful night. The fog seeped into the marrow of your bones and curled in great, fat snakes over the cobblestones as a passing hackney cut a passage through the yellow, choking sea. Everything smelled of fog. The bakery at the corner was baking loaves from fog; the sweetshop was selling sugar mice, licorice laces, Dutch clogs, bull's-eyes, sherbet suckers, and striped humbugs—and all made out of candied fog. Bacon was fried in fog and fog had crept inside the milk bottles to float on the top of the cream in a layer of scum.

The portals of Westerman's loomed up in a forbidding abandon-hope-all-ye sort of way. The fog had arrived at the office before Polly, and Mr. Baines's cadaverous face loomed up out of the gloom. He gave Polly a smile that was more like a grimace.

Amy Feathers scuttled off into the gloom of the upstairs with her shoulders hunched. Bob Friend climbed up onto his high stool, looking sheepish and miserable.

Work at Westerman's had begun again.

Never had Polly worked so diligently or so well.

Somewhere in the pit of Mr. Baines's spirits arose the thought that life might have a few gloomy pleasures left for him, and each energetic tap of Polly's typewriter seemed to hammer away a few of the bitter memories for her.

Amy Feathers felt that each signal from her small switchboard, with its commanding buzzing summons, was life giving her the raspberry, and she fantasized that Polly Marsh had just dropped dead of a heart attack. She, Amy, would of course weep a few tactful tears over the beautiful corpse. Polly's body was being carried out of the office into the fog. *'Forgive me, Amy,'* Bob Friend was sobbing. *'The poor girl is gone but I am so happy to realize that you are the girl I have loved all along!'* And she would cradle his curly head on her thin bosom and whisper . . .

'Miss Feathers!'

Amy was so absorbed in her splendid dream that she was immensely shocked to turn around and find a very alive Polly Marsh standing behind her.

'What is it?' snapped Amy, savagely plugging in a call as if she were sinking a knife into Miss Marsh's delectable bosom.

'Do you think I could possibly telephone Lady Blenkinsop?' asked Polly.

'Personal calls not allowed,' said Amy, adding spitefully, 'and that goes for calls to Buckingham Palace as well.'

A faint sigh escaped Polly. 'You have every reason to dislike me, Amy,' she said in a low voice. 'I have not been very kind to you. But I did not realize until recently that you were in love with Mister Friend.'

Now, no rejected lover wishes to be told that the heart she is wearing on her sleeve has been broadcasting its sad message to all and sundry. Amy turned on Polly in a fury.

'I have no time to listen to your half-witted personal remarks, Miss Marsh. Please return to your duties and stop wasting my time, or I shall be obliged to report you to Mister Baines.'

Polly trailed miserably away into the gloom of the foggy office. She was soon replaced by Bob Friend.

'Amy,' he whispered to Amy's rigid back. 'I'm awfully sorry ... about that night, I mean. I wasn't really thinking of Polly.'

''Course you were,' said Amy with a shrill laugh. 'But don't worry. I was thinking of another chap myself. I was thinking of my fellow, Jim Cooper. We've been walking out together for ever so long.'

Bob Friend felt himself becoming furious. 'Then you had no right to let a chap hold you and kiss you if you're promised to another bloke.'

'Well, you were thinking of Polly.'

'No, I was not. It was a slip of the tongue, that's all,' said Bob angrily. 'You're the one that's to blame ... playing fast and loose with a chap's affections.'

'How dare you,' screamed Amy as the switchboard buzzed an angry counterpoint.

163

'You and your *old school friend*, Polly Marsh.'

'That's different,' said Mr. Friend unforgivably. 'She's so pretty, you can't blame a fellow for wanting to take her to lunch.'

'And I'm so ugly, I'm expected to serve you your blasted lunch at the switchboard!'

'Why you little cat,' hissed Bob.

'You bounder.'

'Shrew!'

'Cad!'

'What *is* all this noise about?' Mr. Baines stood surveying the angry pair. 'Go back to your work, Mister Friend and, Miss Feathers, I have been trying to put a call through.'

Bob Friend scurried off and Mr. Baines turned back to Amy. 'Now, Miss Feathers, please telephone Putney twelve for me and put it through to my receiver downstairs.'

Mr. Baines returned to his desk and sat looking at the black phone with a mixture of excitement and dread. It gave a faint tinkle and he snatched up the heavy receiver and put the earpiece to his ear. 'Hullo,' bellowed a voice at the other end with enough force to crack the vulcanite. The Blenkinsop butler, Wilkins,

164

considered the telephone an unnatural invention in the first place and in the second, he firmly believed that he had to make his voice carry all the way from Putney to the City of London by sheer volume.

'May I speak to Lady Blenkinsop,' whispered Mr. Baines.

'Beg parding?'

'MAY I SPEAK TO LADY BLENKINSOP?'

There was a sudden silence in the office and Mr. Baines could almost see everyone's ears getting larger and larger.

'There h'is no need to shout,' said Wilkins coldly. 'Eh will h'acertain whether her ladyship is at home. What name shall eh say.'

'Baines.'

Mr. Baines pressed the earpiece harder against his ear. Somewhere in the distance he could just distinguish the pompous rumble of the butler's voice and then a high, sweet voice that made his pulse race, then the heavy tread of Wilkins making his way back to the phone.

''Er ladyship h'is not at 'ome—home,' declared Wilkins in stentorian accents. Mr. Baines flushed miserably and put the earpiece back on its hook. He became aware of Polly standing beside him with a sheaf of letters and, looking up, he saw the reflection of his own stricken eyes in the expression in Polly's wide blue ones.

*Why ... she's suffering as well*, he thought. He cleared his throat. 'I have several business matters to discuss and, as I notice the lunch hour has arrived, I wondered whether you would care to join me?'

Polly nodded and went off to collect her coat. Soon both were making their way through the fog to the cosy warmth of Spielmann's. Bloggs and Mr. Baines's other friends watched him, their admiration knowing no bounds.

Mr. Baines was trying to relive his first lunch with Lady Blenkinsop. He ordered the same food and the same wine. But all it did was accentuate his feeling of loss and his eyes filled with unmanly tears. Polly stared at him in dismay and somewhere in her mind came an echo of the marquis's voice telling her it was better to talk away the hurt.

She placed a sympathetic hand on Mr. Baines's arm (Bloggs choked into his beer) and said in a soft voice, 'It's better to tell *someone*, Mister Baines. Is it about Lady

Blenkinsop? You must forgive me. I couldn't help hearing . . .'

Mr. Baines looked into her warm, sympathetic eyes and began to talk. What an agony of love, passion, pain, rejection, and loss came pouring out in the staid confines of Spielmann's. With a new maturity Polly realized that she could ease a lot of her own pain by helping someone else.

She said cautiously, 'Perhaps you do not wish me to interfere, Mister Baines, but Lady Blenkinsop asked me to call on her at any time. Maybe if I visited her, I could convey a message or let her know how you feel . . .'

'*Would you?*' breathed Bertie Baines.

'Of course,' smiled Polly. 'But you must ask Amy to get the call for me. I am not allowed personal calls.'

'Certainly! Certainly!' said Mr. Baines, cracking his knuckles. 'Are you finished? Good! Let us go to the switchboard immediately.'

Amy dutifully asked the operator to get Putney twelve but not before she had cast Polly a withering look. Amy believed that Polly had reported her to Mr. Baines, and once more in her mind the lifeless corpse of

Miss Marsh was borne from the office.

★     ★     ★

The Marquis of Wollerton was hunched in an armchair in his club. He could not get Polly Marsh out of his mind and it was all he could do to stop himself from rushing down to Westerman's.

Hadn't his mother just been congratulating him on the fact that that 'terrible little Marsh girl' was gone from their lives? He frowned unseeingly at his crisply ironed newspaper. He really must either *do* something or put the girl from his mind entirely. Her memory was spoiling the even tenor of his day. He suddenly thought of Lady Blenkinsop. *She* had seemed sympathetic toward the girl. It would do no harm to call in at Putney . . . just a social call of course. Perhaps he might even hear something that would put him off the girl entirely. After all, she was an absolute outsider.

★     ★     ★

The heavy gray clouds seemed to crouch in a threatening mass behind the Blenkinsop mansion as Polly once again pushed open the heavy iron gates. The bitter wind hissed across the surface of the Thames throwing up little whitecaps on its black surface and turning the broad sweep of the river into a stormy and miniature Atlantic, with the corpses of dead trees holding up their branches above the winter water, as if appealing for help to a race of ancient and uncaring gods.

Polly was wearing the serge dress, which felt thin and inadequate against the bite of the wind. All the fog had been ruthlessly sponged from it leaving it only a limp memory of its former warm glory.

Lady Blenkinsop was reclining on a chaise longue in the sitting room. Two patches of rouge stood out sharply on her thin white face and she raised a thin, skeletal arm in a gesture of welcome as Polly was ushered into the room.

'Oh, my lady,' gasped Polly. 'What *is* the matter?'

'I am going into a decline, I think,' said Lady Blenkinsop, with a flash of her old humor. 'I have another guest arriving so please tell me your news first.'

'I am worried about Mister Baines,' said Polly simply. 'He seems to be grieving.'

A blush swept over Lady Blenkinsop's thin face. 'There's nothing I can do about it,' she said in a painful whisper. 'I am a married lady, my dear, and, in society, we are only allowed to have our little affairs until we are found out.'

'But surely you must *feel* something,' said Polly, aware that she was being impertinent but determined to have some news with which to console Mr. Baines.

'Tell Bertie,' she said, 'that I shall always remember him with affection. But nothing more. Nothing more.'

'I'm sorry to upset you, my lady,' said Polly, 'but—' She broke off as the Marquis of Wollerton was announced.

Polly and the marquis stared at each other in dismay. The marquis made a little gesture, almost as if to leave, when he heard Lady Blenkinsop saying weakly, 'My dear Marquis, you must forgive me. I feel quite faint.

'Tell Wilkins to send my maid to me and please show Miss Marsh the conservatory. I shall be quite well presently.'

After Wilkins had been sent on his errand, Polly and the marquis entered the suffocating heat of the conservatory and stared in silence at the plants. The hum of the steam heating system underlined the hot and heavy silence. Far above the glass roof the gray clouds tumbled across the winter sky, driven by a rising wind.

'They are splendid plants,' said the marquis pleasantly.

'Y-yes,' stuttered Polly. 'Very green, aren't they?'

'Very green,' agreed the marquis. 'And so *leafy*.'

'W-what a l-lot of glass.'

'Yes. Isn't it. And so glassy.'

Polly gave him a fulminating look. 'You are teasing me.'

'Yes,' he replied gently. 'I am talking nonsense to stop myself from taking you in my arms.'

Immediately he wished he had not said anything so provocative. Polly was looking at him wide-eyed. He was aware of his own strong desire, almost as if strong cords of desire were stretching out from his body to draw her closer.

She edged away from him, further and further, until the small heels of her button boots were pressed against the edge of a goldfish pond in the center of the conservatory.

Polly stared up at the pale golden eyes as

the marquis came close to her. Her legs felt weak and trembly but she knew she must not let him touch her. Still staring at him as if mesmerized, she took a step backward—and landed with a splash in the warm water of the goldfish pond.

She struggled to get up. The marquis leisurely stepped into the pond as if he were in a drawing room and knelt down in the water beside her. Slowly his arms went around her and held her close, and his lips found hers and both floated away on a silent tide of passion, unaware that they were lying together in the middle of Lady Blenkinsop's conservatory and in the middle of Lady Blenkinsop's goldfish pond. His kisses were searching and exploring and Polly realized for the first time in her young life what it is to want a man with every fiber of your being. Still kissing her, he opened the tiny buttons at the front of her dress and then drew back and looked down at her magnificent breasts lying white and gleaming under the green water of the pond. He caressed them gently and bent his head to hers again, feeling the weedy taste of the water against his lips and then feeling almost nothing but an uncontrollable passion.

'Tea is served.'

The voice of Wilkins came from the direction of the conservatory door.

The marquis swore and sat up. Polly became aware for the first time since he had kissed her that she was lying among the weeds of the pond and that curious goldfish were nibbling at her hair.

Shielding Polly from Wilkins's protruding stare—so very like that of the disturbed goldfish—the marquis snapped, 'Tell Lady Blenkinsop that we shall both need to borrow dry clothes. We both had an accident and fell in the pond.'

'Quite, my lord,' said Wilkins, his face an impassive mask.

*　　*　　*

'So tell me all the London gossip,' said Lady Blenkinsop, looking curiously over the tea things at the odd couple in front of her. The marquis was dressed in one of Sir Edward Blenkinsop's tweed suits. It was miles too wide for him and miles too short. Polly was wearing one of Lady Blenkinsop's wool dresses that was miles too long and miles too small in every other direction.

The marquis chatted away pleasantly while Polly felt waves of shame washing over her. She must have been mad! Bad enough to have submitted to his caresses like any common miss—but in a goldfish pond?

Polly shared the religious beliefs of Stone Lane. If you sinned—and all pleasures were sinful—then God would punish you. You had to pay for what you got in your spiritual life as well as in the earthly life of Stone Lane. Having absolutely no inkling of the facts of life, Polly began to fear that she might become pregnant, and her face became whiter and whiter. Surely the intimate caresses she had allowed were as far as *anyone* could go. Why, she had been almost naked to the waist!

Polly sat in agonized silence over her untasted tea and at last became aware that Lady Blenkinsop was ordering the marquis to drive her home. Polly made a few incoherent noises meaning that she would return home alone but nobody understood her and she soon found herself alone with the marquis in his carriage.

He immediately tried to take her in his arms again but she shrank from him as if he were some species of poisonous reptile.

'Keep away from me,' she gasped.

'I don't understand you,' he said testily. 'One minute you're swooning in my arms and the next you're backing off as if I've got the pox.'

'Oh, the shame of it,' sobbed Polly, bursting into tears. 'I'm ruined!'

'Rubbish!' said the marquis nastily.

Polly sobbed harder. 'In a goldfish pond,' she wailed. 'It's not natural!'

'Balderdash! What do you consider natural? I know. Furtive fumblings in bed with all the lights out.'

Shock dried Polly's tears. He had mentioned bed. She must be pregnant. Her face grew very white indeed.

The marquis suddenly became concerned. 'You look frightened to death. What on earth is troubling you?'

'What if I am pregnant?' There! She had said it.

The marquis tried hard not to laugh. 'How on earth could you possibly be pregnant?' he asked gently.

Polly bowed her head and whispered, 'I had no clothes on from the waist up.'

'Well, my dear,' he said in the same gentle tones, 'it's when you are naked from the waist down that you have something to

175

worry about.'

A mental picture of Polly naked from the waist down made Sir Edward Blenkinsop's short suit seem suddenly unbearably short in the wrong places. He closed his eyes and reached out his hands.

But Polly was immersed in the relief that she had done nothing to endanger her virginity. Never would she make such a mistake again! She had let her wicked senses and thoughts of lust lead her astray. Decent women did not feel like that. She looked at the marquis with his closed eyes and stretching hands and jerked open the carriage door as they slowed in the press of Putney traffic.

The marquis felt the cold wind on his face and opened his eyes. The carriage door was swinging open and the snow whirled and danced but of Polly Marsh, there was no sign at all.

## CHAPTER TEN

Winter had settled his icy grip on London. Snow fell heavily for two days, flying in white sheets across the City, and Polly, trudging homeward in the freezing cold and press of equally cold businessmen, felt gloomily as if time had played some awful trick on her and that she were taking part in the retreat from Moscow.

Snow pitilessly covered the human bundles of rags lying in doorways and froze innumerable families to death in their East End tenements.

The New Year dawned grim and white, a glittering extension to the kingdom of winter, where no bird sang and human souls and human emotions seemed frozen by the cold and the incredible effort of getting to and from work.

Fear of unemployment drove the working masses into the City in droves in the morning, stumbling and falling over the drifts, almost dreading the warmth of their offices, which would only mean the painful return of life to numbed hands and feet.

In a bitter way, Polly was glad of the cold; glad of the battle of the elements that kept feelings at bay and made thoughts of love amongst the goldfish a mad and distant memory.

Then the frost came, bitter, biting hoar frost that glazed the windows of Westerman's with fantastic flowers, burst the mains in the roads, and removed a good lot more of the unwanted poor from the face of the earth.

The austere discipline of Westerman's was relaxed as the staff exchanged horrendous stories about their various safaris across ice-bound London.

*     *     *

Alf Marsh felt weary and chilled to the bone. Sometimes there were no vegetables to buy at Covent Garden Market after his early morning trudges through the snow. The whole of the south of England was in the grip of winter, and often the ships with their cargoes of produce from warmer climates were delayed by the awful weather.

He was shivering looking over his meager stock and was just about to call it a lost day when he became aware that a tall, elegantly dressed swell was standing in the dark doorway of the shop against the blinding backdrop of the snow outside.

Alf scurried forward, rubbing his numb fingers. 'Can I 'elp yer nibs?' he said cheerfully. 'Ain't got much.'

The thin white face of the stranger stared

at him curiously from under the brim of a tall silk hat. Alf's quick eyes traveled over the tall figure. Frogged beaver coat, pigskin gloves, gold-topped cane. Alf's face hardened. One of the nobs out slumming. Out to pick and poke and insult for Gawd knows what pleasure. The stranger remained silent.

'If you don't want nuffink,' said Alf, ''op it!'

The stranger smiled. 'I am Wollerton—Edward, Marquis of Wollerton, and you, I believe, are Mister Marsh, Polly's father.'

'Ho!' said Alf. 'Friend o' Polly's. Well, what abaht it?'

The marquis closed his eyes slightly, drew a deep breath, and said, 'Would you do me the inestimable honor of presenting me with a . . . stone of potatoes.'

Alf looked at him in amazement. 'All right, yer ludship. Potatoes is abaht all I've got—this bleedin' weather.'

Alf scurried off to pile the potatoes on the scale. *Wot's 'e want?* he thought to himself. *Gent like 'im talking abaht potatoes and bein' a friend o' Pol's. Maybe 'e wants 'em free!*

But he kept his thoughts to himself.

'Anyfink else?' he asked brightly.

'Yes,' said the marquis desperately. 'I
179

would like ... deem it a great honor ... oh, five pounds of turnips, please.'

'Turnips it is,' said Alf faintly. He wished his wife were here. She would know what to do. Then he remembered that this was the marquis who had taken his wife to tea at the Ritz. Should he mention it?

'Look, dash it all,' said the marquis. 'What I really want to ask you is—'

'Didn't you entertain my missus to tea?'

'Yes,' said the marquis abruptly, and then repeated 'yes' in a milder voice. 'I enjoyed her company immensely.'

'Beg pardon, yer ludship,' said Alf, 'but these 'ere turnips is big. Get abaht two weighing five pounds.'

'That's all right,' said the marquis. He paused and looked down into Alf's innocent, sparkling eyes. Alf rubbed his grimy mittened hands. He envisaged presenting Alf to his mother. He shuddered.

'Anyfink else?' asked Alf helpfully.

The marquis looked wildly around the small, dark shop. 'Give me everything you've got,' he said.

'Naow then, naow then,' said the amazed Alf. 'Seeing as how yer ludship is in the way of being a friend of the family, like, I feels I

180

'*as* to tell yer that all that there stuff ain't as fresh as it could be, wot with there being nothing ahrand the Market these days.'

'It doesn't matter,' said the Marquis, suddenly desperate to get away and noticing that Alf Marsh was showing every sign of meticulously weighing every vegetable in the shop. 'Just wrap it up.'

'Wot? The 'ole shop full?'

'Yes. I'll call the servants. Load it in the carriage and—here.' He pulled out his purse. 'Here is twenty guineas. That should cover it.'

Alf stared at the gold as if he could not believe his eyes. Times had been hard recently for the Marsh family because of the lack of sales. But Alf Marsh could not cheat.

'Look, yer ludship,' he said in a kindly voice—as if talking to one of the wild young traders down at the pub when one of them tipsily tried to buy drinks for everyone— 'put yer money away. There ain't one guinea's wurrf in the 'ole lot.'

'Take it, man! Take it!' said the marquis, putting the money down on the scale. His puzzled servants were already loading the fruit and vegetables into the carriage.

'I am delighted to have made your

181

acquaintance, Mister Marsh,' said the marquis as correct as ever. 'Please convey my best regards to Mrs. Marsh and to Polly.'

He bowed and left. Alf Marsh turned slowly and stared at the small pile of gold bobbing on the scales.

'Cor lumme,' he said. 'Stone the bleedin' crows.'

A turnip rolled across the carriage and nudged the marquis on the foot. It looked like a great blind head.

'Damn Polly Marsh,' said the marquis. 'I must be mad.'

★   ★   ★

Polly paused at the foot of the stairs and sniffed. Delicious, exotic smells were floating down from the Marshs' flat—smells of goose and roasting chestnuts and plum sauce and crackling-hot roast potatoes and sage-and-onion stuffing.

Polly's chilblained feet flew up the stairs. She crashed open the kitchen door.

The small kitchen was crammed not only with her family but with what seemed like every single old-age pensioner in Stone Lane. Amid a reverent silence Alf was mixing a rum punch, his wrinkled apple of a face gleaming with pleasure. Mrs. Marsh had her sleeves rolled up and was basting a huge goose in the oven.

A large glazed ham glittered on the table, cheek by jowl with an enormous game pie with raised pastry. A small barrel of oysters was being prized open by Gran, and Joyce was removing a giant fruit cake from its tin box, on top of which Queen Victoria was portrayed holding out her chubby little hands in benediction over the feathered head of a Zulu chief and, from the look on her face, not enjoying the occasion one bit.

Polly wanted to scream, 'Where? What? How?' but the silence was almost religious as the old people, who could not remember their last decent meal, gazed with wide eyes on the glory and splendor of the feast.

She silently took a tray of glasses of punch from her father and passed them around. There was a universal sigh of satisfaction as rum and sugar and lemon and boiling hot water seeped into old bones and frozen feet.

Then it seemed as if everyone began to talk at once.

Polly stood bewildered, listening to the incoherent babble. Some lord had thrown a handful of diamonds at her father. He had come in a gold carriage bedecked with rubies, and black servants had cleared a path through the snow for him with silver shovels. He had been wearing knee breeches and the Order of the Garter. 'Wot! In this weather? Garn!') He had been dressed in scarlet and ermine. He had been wearing a crown. It wasn't a lord but King Edward himself!

The arrival of the goose silenced the company again and nothing was heard for half an hour but the chomping of worn teeth and gums. Overcome by all the excitement and having been accidentally handed a glass of punch, little Alf put his small head in his plate and went to sleep.

Polly at last managed to ask her mother what it was all about as they began to clear away the empty and polished plates. She listened wide-eyed as she heard of the marquis's visit and of the gold.

''E's either balmy or 'e's in love with yer, Pol,' said Mrs. Marsh. 'An' I think it's love. Yerse.'

Polly blushed as the memory of the goldfish pond rushed into her mind. She felt obscurely threatened. She was frightened over the intensity of her feelings.

Better never to see or hear of the marquis again.

'Anyways,' Mrs. Marsh continued, 'your father, saint that 'e is, says to me, 'e says, "Let's give all them old folks a treat."'

'Gawd 'elp us, Pol. We've got our 'ealth and strength to last this winter but not them.'

After the last of the guests had gone, clutching their food parcels made up from the remainder of the feast and a little purse of money each, Polly climbed the stairs to her room and stood for a long time looking out at the frozen snow.

To think of the marquis was wrong. All it ever brought was trouble.

Oh, why couldn't he have stayed away!

★　　　★　　　★

The evenings grew longer but still the trees held their leafless branches up to the sky and still the iron grip of winter kept its grim hold on the land.

The marquis was just indulging in a dream in which he had completely managed to forget both Polly Marsh's face and figure. He was promenading along Jermyn Street on his way to his club in St. James's

185

when he almost collided with a trim figure emerging from the back door of Fortnum & Mason. 'Sally Saint John,' he cried with surprise.

A pair of roguish blue eyes twinkled up into his, reminding him of his salad days when he used to squire Sally to balls and go rowing at weekends with her brother, Jerry.

'I'm not Saint John anymore,' she laughed. 'You *are* out of touch. I'm married to Freddie Box.'

The marquis dimly remembered Lord Freddie Box as being a slightly pimply youth in his form at Eton. He must have blossomed indeed to have snared the fair Sally.

'And Jerry's getting married too,' Sally bubbled on. 'And to a little actress from the Gaiety!'

'Good God!' said the marquis. 'What has your mama to say about that?'

'Oh, nothing *now*,' said Sally cheerfully. 'But how she ranted and raved when Jerry first told her. So at last she had to meet the girl; Alice James is her name. Well, the fair Alice turned out to be a very proper young lady, with the manners and voice of a duchess, and Mama was so relieved she gave them her immediate blessing.'

'It sounds almost too good to be true,' said the marquis gloomily.

Sally observed him with interest. 'My dear Edward,' she exclaimed at last. 'You are not by any chance contemplating a *mésalliance* yourself! Not the fastidious Edward! Not the breaker of hundreds of hearts!'

The marquis looked at her with some embarrassment. 'The lady I am "contemplating" is merely a young friend of quite low birth. She is however a very refined young lady. I do not intend to marry the girl or anyone else for that matter, but it does seem a shame that she should wilt away in the East End of London instead of enjoying some West End society.'

'Like my salon, of course,' said Sally brightly.

'Like your salon,' said the marquis smoothly.

'I shall probably regret this,' said Sally gloomily. 'Give me her address, Edward, and I'll send her a card. You will be present of course?'

'Of course,' said the marquis with a grin.

But as it turned out, Lady Sally Box's

pretty salon was not fated to be graced by the plebeian beauty of Miss Polly Marsh.

Sally handed the marquis a letter that he studied in silence. It said: 'Miss Polly Marsh thanks Lady Sally Box for her kind invitation to tea but regrets that she is unable to attend.'

The marquis swore under his breath. He would never see her again unless he hung around Westerman's or visited her home.

Hell and damnation! It looked as if he would have to marry her after all!

★ ★ ★

Fortunately for the marquis, it was not Alf Marsh who was presiding over the dark, chilly shop but Mary Marsh.

Mrs. Marsh wasted no time on social pleasantries. 'Before you feels obliged to buy up the 'ole shop agin,' she said, her small eyes twinkling, 'just gits to the point. Yer wants to marry Pol, doncher?'

The marquis gave a stately nod of his head.

'Well, yer can't,' said Mrs. Marsh brusquely and then her voice softened. 'Sit down 'ere, me lord, and I'll tell you why.'

A savage winter gale was whipping along

Stone Lane and moaning around the gables of the old houses. Its mad, dreamy symphony of summer gone and love lost underlined Mrs. Marsh's explanation. Polly should not marry out of her class, she explained. That sort of thing led to disaster. In vain did the marquis recite lists of his aristocratic friends who had married members of the lower orders; Mrs. Marsh remained adamant. His own mother could not have been more against it. Polly should eventually marry a nice boy in her own station of life. The marquis thought of Polly's gentle beauty under the rough, red, beefy hands of some market trader and felt his temper rising.

Never once had he dreamt of rejection. His fortune was large; his line stretched back into the mists of history. He was accounted handsome. And now he was sitting in some poky little shop in the East End of London being told, in effect, that his proposal of marriage was unwelcome. This is what came of not keeping one's distance! This is what came of fraternizing with the lower orders. Damn this smelly shop, this smelly lane, this dingy environment where the very cobblestones screamed poverty and depression. And

damn Polly Marsh! He gave Mrs. Marsh a
bow as cold and chilly as the day outside
and walked languidly to his motorcar—he
had not wanted the carriage servants to
realize the depths of his infatuation—with
his head held very high and his aristocratic
profile presented to the lower orders. He
felt like a fool.

*     *     *

March came in like a lion and went out like
a monster. The trees on Hampstead Heath
threw down a quantity of branches in
defeat. Winter had come to stay. Icy blasts
all the way from the Arctic circle set the
bare branches of the trees moaning and
rattling like so many skeletons of the
damned.

Winter himself seemed to have taken
over Bertie Baines's heart. Somewhere
outside the kingdom of his frozen and
numbed depression he could hear his wife's
strident voice. Gladys had unfortunately
recovered from the shock of her husband's
affair with Lady Blenkinsop and her voice
rose and fell and moaned like the wind on
the Heath outside. She had sacrificed the
best years of her life to Bertie Baines and

look where it had got her. He never took her anywhere. She had had more fun at her mother's. Why? They had played bridge every evening. Would Bertie Baines play bridge? No! He would not!

On and on it went as Bertie crouched in his armchair, cracking his knuckles and remembering every look and gesture of Lady Blenkinsop's and wondering sometimes if a chap could die from sheer misery.

★    ★    ★

Amy Feathers went out of her way to wait outside the office at closing time so that she could cut Bob Friend dead as he scuttled past.

★    ★    ★

Sir Edward Blenkinsop was seen promenading with the cosy armful from the King's Road on more than one occasion, and everyone vowed to tell Lady Blenkinsop so, but nobody did.

★    ★    ★

A large tear fell on a photograph of the Marquis of Wollerton escorting the beautiful and dashing young Lady Alice Hammersfield to the opera. Polly closed the magazine with a sigh and stared unseeingly out of her window at the black and tumbling clouds. She had not been told of the marquis's proposal. She had refused the mysterious invitation from Lady Sally because her mother had told her to, but she often wondered what would have happened if she had gone.

April brought showers of sleet and hail to the frozen City and people shook their heads and said that the new Ice Age had arrived.

## CHAPTER ELEVEN

Polly Marsh opened her eyes on May the first and was dimly aware that something strange had happened to the world.

Sunlight was flooding the room. She opened the window and leaned out.

Sunshine! Blazing-hot sunshine! Blue sky stretched for miles and miles. Lazy wisps of smoke climbed from chimneys up high into the azure bowl.

A group of jugglers and acrobats were setting out to entertain the streets of the more prosperous West End. The leading acrobat in his tawdry tinsel and faded pink tights suddenly stretched his arms wide and executed several handsprings down the street. Mrs. Benjamin, who lived directly across the lane, opened her window and put her pet linnet, Sammy, out in his wicker cage on the sill. The bird shuffled around ruffling his feathers and then began to pour out a whole song of gladness for the return of spring.

Bernie at the fish-and-chip shop cranked up his new phonograph and soon the tinny, cheeky voice of Marie Lloyd was serenading Stone Lane with Bernie howling in accompaniment.

'My old man said foller 'er van,' roared Bernie.

'And don't dillydally on the way,' caroled Mrs. Marsh from the kitchen downstairs.

'Off went the van wiv 'er 'ole lot in it,' chirped Alf from the shop.

'An' I walked behind wiv me old cock linnet,' shrilled Mrs. Battersby from the tenement next door.

'All tergither now,' shouted a trader from

the street below, leaning on his handcart. And it seemed as if the whole of Stone Lane suddenly burst out singing:

'But I dillied and dallied,
Dallied and dillied,
Lost me way and don't know where to
  roam.
Oh, you can't trust the specials,
Like the old-time coppers
And I can't find my way 'ome.'

The great winter weight of social humiliation, shame, and chilblains whirled around Polly's head, rose up like an evil mist, and melted away in the sunshine.

She took her summer dress out of the closet and shook out its folds. It was of navy-and-white-spotted organza with a high-boned collar and long tight sleeves. By the time Polly had placed a jaunty straw boater on top of her golden curls, she had mentally resolved to say something nice to Amy Feathers. *No wonder Amy dislikes me*, thought Polly. *But I don't care! I'm just going to go on being nice until she likes me.*

What a splendid walk to the City it was. Complete strangers shouted 'good morning.' Message boys whistled as they

194

went about their work, and a few stunted plane trees on the Kingsland Road had burst into delicate green leaf.

The working masses who had trudged to work all winter in a scurrying frozen mass now sauntered gaily in the sunshine, the men flourishing and brandishing their walking sticks and twirling their mustaches as if the warmth of the sunshine had transformed them all into the gayest dashing blades.

It was a Dick Whittington City of London. Everything was paved with gold from the very cobblestones to the gilded roof of St. Pauls.

Polly stood on the threshold of Westerman's, glowing like the morning outside. 'Good morning everyone,' called Polly cheerfully, her light clear voice sailing into every dingy corner of the office like a summer song. And 'Good Morning, Miss Marsh,' chorused the clerks with surprise, noticing for the first time that the stuck-up Miss Marsh was human after all.

Polly sat cheerfully down at her typewriter and waited for Mr. Baines. Suddenly, she was overcome with such a longing for the marquis that her hands began to tremble and she put them under the desk. How could she have ever dreamt that she could forget him? She had not cried over his photograph because she remembered her humiliation at the hands of his brother, but because, she realized, she was in love with him and she was jealous.

★　　★　　★

Mr. Baines wearily stood just inside his front door, the stained glass checkering his face with myriad squares of colored light. He looked like a particularly miserable harlequin.

'And don't forget,' Gladys was saying, 'to bring home a barrel of oysters from Sweetings. Write it down, now.'

'I don't need to write it down,' said Bertie patiently.

'Yes, you do! Yes, you do! You forget everything! Just write it down! Just write it down!'

Mr. Baines meekly took out a small notebook and noted down '1 brl ostrs.' Gladys peered over his shoulder, her very curl papers bristling with irritation. 'What's *that* scriggle-scraggle? Write it proper ... Oh here, let *me* do it. I declare you need a keeper. And don't forget, Mother is coming to dinner and we are making up a four for bridge whether you like it or not.'

'Yes, dear.'

'And here. Let me straighten your tie. I declare if it weren't for me, you'd go to that office looking like a real ragbag.'

The memory of other fingers straightening his tie swept over Mr. Baines and he closed his eyes.

'And just what do you mean by that expression on your face, Bertie Baines?' shrilled Gladys. 'Just what do you mean?'

'I'm tired, my dear.'

'You're tired! *You're* tired! Haven't you any idea of the amount of slaving and scrimping I have to do to see that we keep up a proper appearance? Not that you care for appearances. Ho, no!'

And Mr. Baines opened the door.

And Mr. Baines stood stock-still and stared.

A sea of delicate green flowed from the edge of the Heath all the way to Highgate as the fresh young leaves moved lazily and gently in the warm breeze. The grass rippled and rolled and turned like the fur of some enormous green cat. Forsythia blazed in golden glory beside the garden gate and, on the edge of one of the heavy golden branches, a thrush sang away the memories of the long, dark winter.

On the edge of this other world came the voice of Gladys Baines. 'What are you standing there like a tailor's dummy for?'

Mr. Baines turned around and looked at his wife. He said, 'Shut up, you frightful old bag.'

He tilted his hat to one side of his head. He *jumped* over the garden gate.

The startled thrush flew off to look for a more appreciative audience, and Gladys Baines went home to mother.

★    ★    ★

Lady Blenkinsop sat bolt upright against her lacy pillows, the letter she had just finished reading lying on the quilt. She reached a thin hand toward it and picked up her cup of coffee instead. After all, she knew every word by heart.

It was from her old school friend, Hester Williams. Lady Blenkinsop had not seen Hester in years and could only remember her as a fat, gossipy schoolgirl, much given to sniggering in corners. The letter was to

inform her 'dear friend Jennie' that Sir
Edward had been seen on numerous
occasions escorting a certain Lily
Entwhistle. Hester had felt it her
unpleasant duty to shadow the couple—
'just like Sherlock Holmes!'—and had
espied them entering a flat in the King's
Road above a dressmaker's shop. Diligent
inquiries had revealed that Sir Edward was
*paying* for the rent of the cozy flat, and Miss
Lily, herself, was an erstwhile barmaid
from the Potter's Arms. Hester felt sure
that her dear Jennie would know just what
to do!

*But I don't know what to do*, thought
Lady Blenkinsop sadly. *I might have known
last Christmas, but now . . .*

She looked around the room. The
curtains were tightly drawn and the only
light came from a rose-shaded lamp beside
her bed.

She leaned her head back against the
pillows and suddenly became aware that the
birds were singing and squabbling in the
ivy outside.

She moved from the bed with frail,
tentative steps and jerked the heavy curtain
cord.

With her thin hand at the throat of her

lacy negligee, she stared at the sunlit scene laid out in front of her.

The lawns swept down to the edge of the sparkling river. A gaily-painted launch cut a swathe through the perfect mirror of the water, sending little creamy waves lapping against the incredible green of the lawn. Daffodils nodded in the gentle breeze, and pink and white daisies starred the rougher grass near the water's edge. Two noisy whitethroats chased each other through the graceful, swaying branches of a weeping willow.

Against the garden wall a magnificent horse chestnut held its tall spires of blossom to the warmth of the early sun, and a hawthorn covered with a white sheet of flowers brought memories of the winter blizzards.

Lady Blenkinsop opened the window and the stuffy room was filled with the scent of blossom and the sound of birds and lapping water.

She stood for a long time watching the river and then she turned and rang the bell.

Her lady's maid, Withers, answered the bell promptly and showed no surprise or indeed any expression at all when her mistress declared her intention of breakfasting downstairs.

Sir Edward Blenkinsop was spearing the last grilled kidney with his fork when his wife marched into the room. He rose and tried to kiss her on the cheek but her very flesh seemed to cringe from his touch.

He rubbed his hands together and tried to voice his surprise at seeing her on her feet. 'Well, well, well,' he said and then added for witty emphasis, 'yes, yes, yes, yes, yes.'

'The sunshine has made me feel *much* stronger, Edward,' said Lady Blenkinsop pleasantly. 'I may even venture out. Perhaps I may even go as far as the King's Road.'

The veins on Sir Edward's temples began to throb. 'Harrumph ... grumph,' he remarked intelligently.

'Perhaps I may even try that dressmaker's ... you know the one. You pay the rent of a little flat there, don't you dear? A Miss Entwhistle, I believe?'

'Hah, hah, ha! Harrumph,' said Sir Edward.

'Well, let us not fence any longer,' said Lady Blenkinsop, helping herself to toast. 'I know all about Lily. I am suing for a divorce.'

Sir Edward burst into intelligible speech. 'Ho! Hoity-toity. Pot calls the kettle black, what! People in glass houses shouldn't throw stones, what!'

'And every cloud has a silver lining,' said his wife coldly. 'If you do not contest the divorce, dear Edward, I shall pay you an enormous amount of money . . . more than enough to keep twenty Lilys.'

'Well . . . all right,' said her husband, getting to his feet. 'I only married you for your money anyway.'

'I know.'

'Well, well, well.' Sir Edward turned in the doorway, searching desperately for some splendid last words. He found them. 'I never liked you anyway, Jennie, so, yah, yah!'

'Yah, yah to you, too,' said Lady Blenkinsop mildly. 'And close the door after you, please.' He did so with a loud bang. Lady Blenkinsop walked to the morning room window and waited until the brougham bearing her husband had clattered down the drive and out of sight.

She gave a great sigh of relief. She was very lucky. After all, it is not every woman who can stand at the window of her home and watch the source of her illness bowling out of her life forever.

*   *   *

A mischievous summer breeze escaped from the countryside and blew past Amy Feathers as she sat at the switchboard.

Winter had gone and with it all her hurt. She felt ashamed of herself. She had been really nasty to Bob Friend. As the long-forgotten smells of summer—fresh grass, leaves, and blossoms—floated past her little nose, she desperately began to wonder if she had been too cold—too cruel.

She had left herself with nothing. She missed his friendly smile, she missed their lunches together, and she could still feel the pressure of his lips on hers.

She must make up for lost time. She, Amy Feathers, would summon up all her small stock of courage and ... and ... she would wait for him outside the office and ask him to walk her home and pray to God that he would not refuse.

*   *   *

The Marquis of Wollerton opened one yellow eye that splendid morning and asked his man what the hell he was doing bustling and fussing.

His gentleman's gentleman replied with the long-suffering expression he had acquired of late that 'we were packing his lordship's clothes, as we were leaving for France.'

'Of course,' said the marquis wearily. He lay back on the pillows and closed his eyes. In the winter of yesterday it had seemed like such a splendid idea—to put the breadth of the English Channel between himself and Polly Marsh.

His gentleman's gentleman drew the heavy curtains and left, shutting the mahogany door behind him with infuriating gentleness—which is the wellbred servant's way of screaming.

The marquis swung his feet out of bed and padded to the window. The small patch of garden behind his town house in Albemarle Street seemed to have blossomed overnight. It was like magic! The buds and the young leaves must have been flourishing there under the icy lash of the April storms, but he had never noticed them. In a clear blue puddle in the middle of the lawn, a cheeky family of sooty sparrows were squabbling and splashing. A lilac tree, heavy with blossom, moved gently in the breath of the wind. In a nearby house, some child was laboring over Strauss waltzes and Czerny exercises. How poignant is the stumbling music of the amateur heard from a comfortable distance on a sunny morning in May!

Memories and desire came flooding back: Polly catching the red-hot penny; Polly sweeping out of Brown's Hotel; Polly lying in his arms in the goldfish pond, her wet hair spreading out like some exotic weed in the green water, while the startled goldfish glinted and flashed.

It suddenly came to him that he was simply not going to be able to forget her or live without her.

He, who was famous for his success with women, had gone about the whole business liked a callow youth. He had never tried to woo her; he had merely grabbed. He had let overdeveloped class consciousness cloud the whole affair—he who had never cared before what anyone thought of his actions.

Well, he would wait outside the portals of Westerman's at closing time like the veriest stage-door Johnny. And he would force her to listen to him. No. That was wrong. He would coax her to listen to him.

He rang the bell. 'Browning,' he said to the impassive face of his gentleman's gentleman, 'we are not going to France.'

'Very good, my lord.'

'We are going to endeavor to be married.'

'Indeed, my lord. May I offer you my premature congratulations.'

'You have always the *mot juste*, Browning.'

'Quite, my lord.'

'Will you inform the travel agency that ... No, on second thought, I'll inform them myself.'

'Very good, my lord,' said Browning.

'And Browning, I would like to apologize for my somewhat autocratic behavior during the past few months. I have had many worries.'

'Very good, my lord,' said Browning, again closing the door with an infuriating silence, for, as he confided to the butler downstairs, 'Apologies is one thing. Actions is another.' And no one could deny that the long-nosed, white-faced bleeder had been merry hell to work for during the winter.

★　　★　　★

206

The marquis was strolling along Piccadilly toward the offices of Thomas Cook and Son when he espied a familiar figure. Lady Blenkinsop was tripping along happily in the sunshine followed by a footman who was burdened with purchases.

He swept off his hat and made her his best bow, although embarrassing memories of the goldfish pond brought a faint flush to his thin face.

'I have finally and definitely managed to remove dear Edward from my life,' began Lady Blenkinsop without preamble. 'Isn't it splendid! I'm celebrating by buying . . . oh! . . . lots and lots of pretty things.'

Her face was still haggard but her eyes sparkled as she looked up at the tall figure of the marquis. They chatted easily for some minutes, although neither of them mentioned Westerman's.

Eventually the marquis said, 'I must get to the travel office to cancel my bookings. I had planned to go to France but I have changed my mind at the last minute.'

Lady Blenkinsop looked at him with interest. 'Really! What a pity to waste the reservations. How many of you were going?'

'Just myself and my man, Browning.'

Lady Blenkinsop felt her heart beginning to pound as a daring idea sprang into her mind. 'My dear Marquis. What a pity to cancel them. I will buy them from you. I had been planning to take a holiday with a . . . a friend.'

The marquis handed her the packet.

'Then have them by all means. My present, I assure you. No, no! I insist.'

But as Lady Blenkinsop's trim figure moved off along Piccadilly, the marquis looked thoughtfully after her. She had always shown a fondness for Polly. He suddenly hoped that Polly was not the friend Lady Blenkinsop was taking to France.

## CHAPTER TWELVE

The blue spring light hung at the corners of the winding City streets. Far away across the river, Big Ben bonged out six golden notes releasing all the City slaves from directors to the office boys out into the mellow, incredible evening.

Mr. Baines neatly cleaned his steel pen and put it in the brass stand on the desk.

He took out the sheet of stained blotting paper and replaced it with a fresh one. He removed his cardboard wristband protectors and rose wearily to fetch his jacket. He felt disappointed.

He could not say why he felt disappointed. All day he had been feeling like a child on Christmas morning. All day he had been sure that something really tremendous had been going to happen. It was there waiting for him, he had been sure, something absolutely marvelous hovering on the edge of the golden day. But work had gone on as usual, a steady progression of bills, letters, invoices, and complaints.

He suddenly could not bear to wait to see that the clerks had completed their work and tidied their desks. He walked to the glass doors of Westerman's and without so much as a 'good-evening' walked outside.

A slim white hand beckoned to him from the window of a heavy traveling carriage.

Bertie Baines hesitated. In his very, very private dreams sometimes a slim hand beckoned just like this one. He walked on.

'Bertie!'

He turned around slowly.

The marquis, leaning languidly against a

pillar at the door of Westerman's, reflected that he had never seen such an ordinary face so transfigured.

His heart beating fast, Mr. Baines ducked his head and plunged into the carriage, to be held by a pair of welcoming arms and enveloped in the almost forgotten aroma of Fleurs d'Antan.

The carriage rattled off.

'Oh, Jennie,' whispered Mr. Baines when he could. 'We should not be doing this.'

Lady Blenkinsop laughed like a very young girl. 'You don't know *what* we are doing Bertie—or rather what I am doing with you. I'm kidnapping you, my dear slave. We're running away to France and you are not going back to Westerman's again.'

'But I *can't*,' yelled Bertie, sitting bolt upright and running his hands through his thin hair until it stood up in spikes. 'I've worked all my life—'

'Think about it,' said Lady Blenkinsop, withdrawing into the far corner of the carriage and turning her head away. 'I can always drive you home any time you wish.'

Bertie thought. And the more he thought of bills and invoices and letters and shipments, the more his life stretched out in front of him as long and as heavy as Marley's chains. Slowly the new idea took over.

What *would* it be like never to work again? What would it be like to see all those fabulous places which up till now had merely been names on a piece of business stationery. What would it be like to hold this woman in his arms every night until the end of time?

He reached out his long, bony arms and grabbed Lady Blenkinsop to his thin chest and then bent his head and kissed her until she was breathless.

'Why Bertie!' she said laughing. 'I believe you're as bad as I am.'

And Bertie Baines stretched out his arms as if to embrace the carriage, the spring evening, the whole world.

'I'm every bit as *good* as you are,' he cried, and began to laugh as the whole novelty of the idea filled his mind. 'I'm every little bit as *good*.'

\*     \*     \*

Amy stood on the worn steps of Westerman's and eyed the Marquis of

Wollerton with dismay. If Bob Friend snubbed her, she did not want *any* sort of audience, particularly this haughty marquis. The ill-assorted pair stood on either side of the steps and each wished heartily that the other would go away.

The door opened and Bob Friend stepped out. He settled his bowler on top of his crisp curls. He said, 'Evening, my lord. Evening, Miss Feathers.' He started to walk away.

'Bob!'

Bob Friend turned slowly. Amy looked piteously from Bob to the marquis and the marquis tactfully turned away.

'Bob,' said Amy desperately. 'Will you walk me home?'

The spring sunlight rushed in from all parts of the dusty City and flooded Bob Friend's soul. 'I'd be delighted to, Miss Feathers,' he beamed. 'Absolutely delighted.'

They stood smiling at one another for a few minutes and then Bob Friend tucked Amy Feather's skinny, birdlike arm confidingly in his own and they both walked off, surveyed by the marquis, who felt a sudden pang of envy.

The couple walked in silence until they

reached the narrow canyon of Fleet Street. 'Would you like a cup of tea before you go home?' asked Bob Friend.

Amy nodded her head, so Bob looked around this world of taverns until he espied a small flyblown tea shop. He pushed open the dingy glass doors and ushered Amy into a small dark room. They sat looking at each other in ecstatic silence until Bob became aware of the reproving stare of a fat, white-faced waiter.

'Two cups of tea,' he ordered dreamily.

'We don't serve cups of tea 'ere,' said the waiter repressively. 'Pots of tea or nuffink.'

'Then bring us a pot of tea,' said Bob, not bothering to look up.

'Sure yer can afford it?'

Bob stared up at the fat face with amazement but before he could speak his outraged beloved had got to her feet. 'What did you say?' said Amy, quivering and bristling like a little cat. 'Less of your sauce, my man. Fetch that pot of tea instanter and take yourself off. Cheek!'

The waiter slouched off and Amy sat down, breathless and triumphant.

Now there is nothing so effective in the sealing of young love as a shared triumph over the petty humiliations of the social

order. The long winter was forgotten, Polly
was forgotten. The clerk and the telephone
girl sat with their hands joined across the
table, king and queen of the oldest
kingdom in the world.

*　　　*　　　*

Polly Marsh looked at the elegant figure of
the Marquis of Wollerton and then looked
down at her boots. She wanted to stay, she
wanted to run away, she didn't know what
she wanted to do.

Feeling ridiculously like Amy Feathers,
the marquis cleared his throat. 'Will you
walk with me for a little, Miss Marsh?'

'Why?'

'Because it is a nice evening for walking.'

'Oh.' Polly looked up at him, irresolute.
He was holding out his arm. She ignored it
and they walked on, each on far sides of the
pavement.

Polly had been late leaving and the City
had already entered its evening quiet. He
was leading her away from her route home,
through various winding lanes, down
toward the river. The lights shone in the
blueish twilight along the Embankment as
the silent pair walked side by side.

'This is ridiculous,' said the marquis finally. 'You know why I want to see you, Polly.'

'Yes,' she answered drearily, looking across the river. 'You want me to go away with you and live in a maisonette in Saint John's Wood, where I will walk my poodle and play bridge with the other ladies of the demimonde.'

'You've been reading too many bad novels,' he remarked, momentarily diverted. 'Some time ago you thought Saint John's Wood a most respectable suburb.'

'It was you who enlightened me,' said Polly crossly.

'Oh, Polly, come and sit down on this bench and listen to me for a minute—'

'You want me to make love to you in goldfish ponds,' said Polly tremulously, sitting down, her back as straight as a ramrod and her straw hat shadowing her face.

'Don't be silly,' said the marquis. 'It may interest you to know that I am not in the habit of making love to ladies under water.'

'Nonsense!' snapped Polly childishly. 'That's probably why you lot go to Cowes . . . so that you can galumph around taking each other's clothes off and prance through

215

the water in the altogether.'

'Don't be vulgar.'

'I *am* vulgar,' said Polly infuriatingly. 'I come from Stone Lane.'

'And never, ever are we going to be allowed to forget it,' said the marquis, with his quick temper beginning to rise.

'And why should I want to forget it?' said Polly, becoming angry herself. 'There's nothing up with Stone Lane.'

'Oh, salt of the earth!'

'Yes, the people in the market *are* the salt of the earth,' said Polly. 'They're kind and generous and—'

'For heaven's sake, girl. I didn't bring you here to listen to you romanticizing a dirty little market.'

'Then why did you bring me here?' howled Polly.

'Because I want to marry you, you cloth-headed little idiot,' he roared.

Both glared at each other, their breath coming quickly.

'Marry ... *you*,' said Polly. 'Why, I wouldn't marry you if ...'

'... if you were the last man alive,' finished the marquis in a mincing falsetto.

'Well, I wouldn't. What's so special about you anyway?'

The marquis was by now so angry he could have beaten her. Who, in the length and breadth of England—provided they are in their right mind—asks a very rich and handsome marquis what's so special about him?

'If you don't see what's so special about me I don't see why I should take the trouble to tell you.'

'I've met some swollen-headed people in my time,' said Polly slowly, 'but you take the biscuit. It must be *killing* you to propose marriage. If you could get me any other way you—'

'You forget. I only make love in goldfish ponds.'

'Any other way, you would not bother to propose.'

'Probably,' said the marquis icily.

Both sat glaring at each other as the sun went down in a blaze of fiery glory. Neither wished to leave before they had crucified the other with some splendid last words.

'To think,' said the marquis finally, 'that I was about to bestow the honor of my name on a little . . . a little typist.'

'Good thing you found out in time,' said Polly with pretended indifference while her very soul throbbed and hurt. 'You know,'

217

she added conversationally, turning and looking full at the marquis, 'if your title and wealth were taken away, you wouldn't really amount to much.'

'If my title and wealth were taken away, my dear girl, you would be falling into my arms instead of letting your peculiar brand of inverted snobbery turn you into an impertinent minx.'

'Any minute now you'll be asking me to remember my place,' blazed Polly.

'Yes, why don't you,' sneered the marquis, looking at her with loathing. He got to his feet. Polly remained motionless, watching him with equal hate as he leaned over the rail and stared at the river. His well-tailored back was almost rigid with distaste and disapproval.

'You know,' he said in a muffled voice, 'I feel I owe you an apology.' Polly's heart leapt but his next words made her blaze again with an uncontrollable fury. 'I thought I loved you. I must have been mad. You! Why, you're nothing but a little . . .'

But whatever biting and cruel words he was about to say were literally drowned by Polly's fury. In one second she had leapt from the bench and delivered a mighty shove to the center of his elegant back.

He somersaulted neatly over the railing into the Thames with hardly a splash and sank like a stone.

Polly clutched the railing and stared down. The marquis's silk hat bobbed jauntily on the muddy water and his cane sailed along beside it. Of the marquis there was no sign at all, and the water turned crimson, like blood in the setting sun.

*I've killed him!* thought poor Polly. The thought that the marquis might have been holding his breath underwater to make her think just that never crossed her mind. With a terrified cry she threw herself bodily over the railing into the Thames. The marquis's head immediately bobbed above the water, like that of a sleek seal. 'Gotcher!' he said with verve worthy of Stone Lane. 'And it serves you right, my girl.'

'I can't swim!' wailed Polly as her straw hat floated away and pursued the marquis's silk hat, which was disappearing in the direction of Greenwich.

Two strong strokes brought him to her side and he pulled her to him. 'You can stand, you know,' he said gently. 'It's low tide.'

Both stood with the oily, muddy waters

of the Thames up to their shoulders and stared at each other.

'Oh, *Polly*,' murmured the marquis, and then he kissed her as ruthlessly and efficiently as he had meant to do all along.

'Wot's all this then?' demanded a stentorian voice from the Embankment. Both broke apart and looked up into the steely, accusing eyes of an officer of the law.

'It's quite all right, Officer,' said the marquis pleasantly. 'I was just rescuing this lady and—'

'Indecent behavior, that's wot it is,' said the constable severely. 'Out of there, both of you.'

With the marquis pushing from behind and the policeman pulling on Polly's outstretched arms, she was landed on the Embankment like a very wet and muddy fish. She stood upright and was soon joined by the dripping-wet marquis, who took her arm in a firm grip.

'Naow, then,' said the policeman, taking out his notebook and licking the end of a stub of lead pencil. 'Let's 'ave yer names.'

'Run for it,' whispered the marquis in Polly's ear.

She needed no second bidding.

''Ere!' roared the policeman. ''Ere!' as the two dripping figures flew along the Embankment. A shrill whistle sounded faintly in their ears as they ran and ran.

The marquis at last jerked Polly into a doorway and they hung onto each other breathless and laughing.

'I think the chase is over,' he said with his lips against her hair. 'We'll find a hack and go to my place and get dried off.'

He felt her stiffen against him and turned her face up to his. 'No more remarks from you, Miss Polly Marsh,' he said severely. 'You are going to marry me and that's that. Now say "yes" like a good girl or I shall be forced to give you a lesson on how to become pregnant right in the corner of this nasty, smelly doorway.'

'Oh, yes,' sighed Polly. 'Yes, I will marry you, Edward . . . but what on earth will my mother say?'

The marquis laughed and held her closer. 'I *know* what *my* mother will say, but no one can do anything about us now, Polly Marsh. We're beyond reclaim.'

\*     \*     \*

Lord Peter stood stock-still at the end of

Albemarle Street and stared at the two familiar figures who were entering an imposing town house. Polly Marsh and his brother! And soaking wet, too!

Now he could get his revenge for that night at Westerman's.

*Mother should be at* her *town house getting ready for the opera*, he thought. *I will just pay her a little call . . .*

## CHAPTER THIRTEEN

The Duchess of Westerman was in a state of baffled fury. She had first had the indignity of being turned away from her elder son's house by his butler's chilly news that 'his lordship is not at home to anyone.' Then her husband had washed his hands of the whole affair, and next she had foregone the opera to travel to this . . . this market to appeal to Mrs. Marsh to find that the good lady and her family had gone out visiting and that Mr. Marsh was in the public house.

Polly's absence had not been noticed. Mrs. Marsh had left her daughter's dinner in the oven and a note pinned to the door to say that she had 'gone to spend the evening at Edie's.'

The duchess had glared at this note and was about to send one of her footmen up and down the lane to find the mysterious Edie's when she decided to vent her wrath on the nearest Marsh available.

The footman was dispatched to the Prince Albert with the stern instructions to bring Mr. Marsh to Her Grace *immediately*.

Her wrath knew no bounds when her footman returned without Mr. Marsh but with the message that Mr. Marsh was enjoying his evening pint of mild and why didn't Her Grace step in and join him.

Wrapped in a white velvet evening cloak and blazing with temper and diamonds, the duchess swept into the Prince Albert and demanded the presence of Mr. Marsh in tones of awesome majesty.

Alf Marsh trotted forward and surveyed the duchess gloomily. They were all bonkers he decided. Any minute now she would be demanding pounds of turnips and stones of potatoes.

'Hah!' said the duchess. 'Well, Marsh, it may interest you to know that your daughter is a fallen woman.'

'Ah, garn!' said Alf in disgust. 'Our Pol's

at 'ome right now, 'aving 'er supper.'

'No, she is not,' said the duchess. 'She is at my elder son the Marquis of Wollerton's house in a state of dishabille.'

''Ere!' exclaimed Alf with alarm. 'I don't think she's been vaxunited.'

'Dishabille is not a disease,' said the duchess crossly. 'I mean that she and my son, in ragged, wet, and muddy clothes, were seen entering his town house, hanging on to each other.'

'Then they probly 'ad an accident,' said Alf. 'My Pol's a decent girl.'

'Hah!' sneered the duchess.

'If you wasn't a lady, I'd punch yer up the froat,' said Alf slowly. All his usual cheerful good humor had left him and he seemed to have grown in stature.

'Now, now,' said the duchess hurriedly, wishing she had asked her footman to accompany her. 'Is there anything to drink in this place?'

'Give the lady a port and lemon,' said Alf over his shoulder, 'and bring it to the private parlor and keep it coming.'

He opened a frosted-glass door and ushered his companion into the private parlor, which was usually used for the local darts teams' war councils.

'Do you expect me to drink that filthy concoction?' demanded the duchess, momentarily diverted as a large glass of port and lemon was placed in front of her.

'Well, why not?' said Alf testily. 'Wot was you a-going to do wiff it otherwise? Polish yer boots?'

The duchess took a large mouthful. It tasted unexpectedly pleasant. 'See here, Mister Marsh,' she said in a more reasonable tone of voice. She took another pull at her glass. 'It is not a question of whether your daughter is seducing my son or whether my son is seducing your daughter, but the fact remains that they are both badly compromised, so what are you going to do about it?'

'Nuffink,' said Alf succinctly. He paused for a minute to watch in amazement as the duchess drained her glass and gulped down another.

'I trust my daughter. I won't believe she's done anything wrong till I sees it wiff my own eyes. So there! And I would advize you to go easy on that there port and lemon. Stronger than yer thinks.'

Just then the barman popped his head around the door. The duchess threw a guinea on the table. 'Keep 'em coming, my

225

good man,' she ordered.

'Right-ho,' said the barman cheerfully, turning a blind eye to Alf's frantic signaling.

*     *     *

Mrs. Marsh rattled her key in the lock and turned to stare at one of the street traders. 'Could you repeat that?' she asked faintly.

''S like I told you,' he said. 'Your old man's along o' the Prince Albert with some great dirty bird all covered in paste, an' she's a-givin' old Alf the glad eye and fillin' 'im up wiff booze.'

'Garn!' said Mrs. Marsh cheerfully. 'The Prince Albert don't allow no brass nails.'

'She's one o' them high-class tarts,' said the trader earnestly. 'Come in a carriage and all, she did. She'll 'ave 'er 'ands on your old man's crown jewels if yer don't 'urry up.'

'Dad ain't got no jewels,' said Joyce, her eyes round with wonder.

Mrs. Marsh sprang into action. 'Gran, take the children upstairs till I go see wot's 'appened.'

She covered the short distance to the Prince Albert with surprising speed. She gave the barman one awful glare and, following the jerk of his head, crashed open the door of the private parlor.

Behind a scarred wooden table covered with dirty glasses sat Her Grace, The Duchess of Westerman. She was crooning softly, and her massive head topped with an elaborate headdress of diamonds and feathers was resting on Alf's small bony shoulder.

'Mary!' gasped Alf. 'Thank Gawd!'

'Who is she?' demanded Mrs. Marsh. 'Them's *real* diamonds.'

'Oh, Mary,' said Alf. 'This 'ere is the Duchess of Westerman wot says our Pol is at 'er son's 'ouse right this minute a-being comporized.'

'Compromised,' said Mrs. Marsh faintly. 'It's that there Marquis of Wollerton, that's wot it is. I told 'im 'e couldn't marry Pol.'

'We'll all go and see Eddie,' said Her Grace, beaming drunkenly. 'All go bye-byes.'

'Right y'are, ducks,' said Mrs. Marsh grimly. 'On yer feet.'

*    *    *

Lord Peter pressed his handsome nose

against the window of Brown's Hotel and gleefully noticed his mother's carriage turning the corner of the street from Piccadilly. He would just be in time to witness his elder brother's humiliation. Whistling cheerfully he left the hotel and trotted along the street just as the carriage arrived outside the marquis's town house. With infinite satisfaction he noticed Mr. and Mrs. Marsh descending from the carriage. With less satisfaction he saw that his mother was weaving along the pavement, supported by two footmen.

Lord Peter gave Mrs. Marsh his best boyish smile. 'Ah, Mrs. Marsh,' he beamed. 'Remember me?'

Mrs. Marsh eyed him from head to foot. 'Yerse,' she said tersely. 'An' I'll be 'aving a word wiff you later, young man.'

Lord Peter quailed but gallantly followed them up the steps. His own philanderings with Polly would surely be forgotten as soon as the redoubtable Mrs. Marsh got her hands on his brother.

The marquis's butler eyed the group on the steps with a well-trained lack of surprise. 'I will ascertain whether his lordship is at home,' he began and gasped as Alf jerked an elbow into his striped

228

waistcoat.

'Stand aside,' bellowed Alf, 'or I'll use yer guts fer garters.'

They had heard the sound of voices from one of the rooms off the hallway. Mrs. Marsh led the way and threw open the door. Four people got to their feet in surprise.

With suppressed fury Peter recognized his brother and Polly together with Lord Freddie Box and his wife, Sally.

The marquis was bowing over Mrs. Marsh's hand. In a soothing voice he was explaining that he and Polly had been splashed by a passing carriage when they had met by chance outside Westerman's. He had telephoned Lady Sally, who had rushed around with a change of clothes for Polly. He was sorry to have caused Mrs. Marsh so much distress, but as Mrs. Marsh could surely see, her daughter was very well indeed.

Mrs. Marsh sank down weakly into a chair. Polly was looking radiant. The duchess was collapsed in another chair. She was crooning faintly.

The marquis took Polly's hand in his. 'Mister and Mrs. Marsh,' he said formally. 'Your daughter has agreed to become my wife. I hope we will have your blessing.'

Mrs. Marsh suddenly felt very, very tired. 'Do you know what you are letting yourself in for, Pol?' she asked.

'Yerse,' said Alf. 'Look at yer future ma-in-law.'

But nothing could penetrate the glass bubble of happiness that surrounded the marquis and Polly. Somewhere outside their happiness Peter sneered, Mr. and Mrs. Marsh fretted and worried, and the duchess sang songs of her childhood in a maudlin voice.

Alf Marsh then protested that, as father of the bride, he could not afford the cost of the wedding. Then they would have a quiet wedding, said the marquis soothingly.

They couldn't have a wedding without inviting all their friends and relatives from Stone Lane, declared Alf triumphantly, and what would his lordship's grand friends think of that?

His lordship answered in tones of utter indifference, that he didn't give a damn what anyone thought about it.

Defeated at last, Mr. and Mrs. Marsh reluctantly gave their blessing.

He escorted the Marshes home, pulling Polly back, as she would have followed her parents into the house. Alf Marsh turned around in the lane to look for his daughter. It had been a long and worrying evening.

'Come along then, Alf,' said Mary Marsh gently. 'Leave 'em alone for a bit. We've got to get used to it. Polly's leaving us. Can't see how we're going to see much of her again.'

And wiping away a tear she went upstairs to hug little Joyce and little Alf with such unwonted fervor that they began to cry and ask whether the Boers had invaded London after all.

## EPILOGUE

The new office manager gave his silk hat a brush with the back of his sleeve and wondered whether houses were haunted after all.

From humble clerk to office manager had been a meteoric rise for Bob Friend. He had married his Amy and, with a generous loan from the bank, had bought Mr. Baines's old house in Hampstead.

That, he reflected, was when all the trouble had started. His thin, vivacious, birdlike Amy had almost immediately started to put on weight. Her voice had taken on a thin, hard veneer of refinement. She saw social snubs at every turn and brooded over them all day, and poured out the accumulated venom of her hurt into her husband's unwilling ears in the evening. She no longer joined him for lunch in case anyone would find out that she once worked as a telephone operator. Bob had once asked one of the clerks and his wife home for dinner and had remarked cheerfully during the evening that Amy used to work for Westerman's. She had never forgiven him.

Amy followed Polly's social career by way of the glossy magazines and wrote frequently to editors reminding them that the Marchioness of Wollerton was nothing more than a cockney office girl. They never replied to her letters.

Bob thought fondly of his new secretary. She wasn't a dazzler like Polly Marsh; she was a quiet little thing with large spectacles and mousy hair scraped back in a bun, but she had a way of saying, 'Oh, *yes* Mister Friend. Of *course* you are right,' which made him feel very masculine and important.

He was toying with the idea of asking her out for lunch as he waited in the hallway to say good-bye to Amy.

Bob turned as his wife came down the stairs heavily. He moved forward to give her a dutiful peck on the cheek. Something in the turn of her head made him remember the old Amy.

'Amy,' he said abruptly. 'I've been standing here thinking about taking my secretary out for lunch. And do you know why? It's because she thinks I'm no end of a great chap, and I'm tired of your putting down and complaining. I'm a decent chap, Amy, but you push me too far.'

Amy felt a chill of terror going through her. She knew she had been awful. She opened her mouth to beg his forgiveness, to say she would change, but instead her voice said, 'Well, go out with your little secretary, for all I care.'

'Very well,' said Bob Friend. He crammed his silk hat on his curls and strode out, slamming the door behind him.

Amy cried for a long time after he had gone. He should have understood her. He should have understood how terrifying it is to cope with servants and snobby shopkeepers and stuck-up neighbors. He

233

should have understood how the loneliness of her days magnified every little irritation.

After a while she dried her eyes and put on her best frock and went to sit in the parlor like the lady she wasn't, wishing heartily that she could do some real old-fashioned dirty housekeeping to occupy her time.

The doorbell rang and Amy went to answer it. The parlormaid was probably taking another morning off and Amy was too frightened of her to rebuke her.

Bertie Baines stood on the doorstep. Both stared at each other with the utmost surprise.

'Amy! What are you doing here?' gasped Mr. Baines.

'I live here,' smiled Amy. 'I married Bob Friend. He got the office manager's job after you left.'

'Good heavens!' said Mr. Baines. 'I was walking across the Heath and I decided to have a look at my old home.'

'Please come in,' said Amy, stepping aside. 'You do look fit.'

Bertie Baines looked fit indeed. He was lean and tanned and wearing a very expensive white raw-silk suit. Amy rang the bell for the tea tray and then bit her lip as she realized that no one would answer the bell.

Bertie quickly assessed the situation. Fancy little Amy Feathers having servants—even though she obviously did not know how to cope with them.

'Perhaps you would care to take a stroll with me, Mrs. Friend,' he said. 'It's a beautiful morning. Now wouldn't it be nice to get out of the house?'

'Oh, yes!' cried Amy, jumping to her feet. She ran lightly up the stairs to fetch her very best hat. She felt sure Mr. Baines would appreciate it.

They walked along by the Heath under the heavy summer trees in companionable silence. Amy felt that she could almost behave like herself and Bertie did not feel obliged to say anything witty or clever.

They found a small tearoom near the High Street, with little tables on the pavement outside, and Bertie Baines drew out Amy's chair for her and then sat down with a sigh of satisfaction.

'I must say it does my heart good to see you, Mrs. Friend. I'm going back into the business world, you know. Got a job as office manager with Westerman's rivals—Heatherington's, you know—they're on the other side of the Bank.'

'But I thought you were . . .' Amy began and then bit her lip.

'You thought I was living in the South of France with a certain lady,' said Bertie Baines. 'Well, I was. But somehow I couldn't fit in. All the nobs there treated me as if I were a very funny joke on the part of Lady—on the part of my lady friend. Some of them mistook me for the butler.'

Amy's tortured and refined accents fled before a wave of pure sympathy. 'Oh, I know what it's like, Mister Baines—trying day in and day out to be something you're not. 'Course, it's easy for some. Take my Bob. He never seems to notice the change. You'd think he'd had servants all his life.'

'Anyway,' said Mr. Baines, taking a swallow of strong tea and helping himself to a large slice of Congress cake, 'it's going to be good to get back into harness.'

'You wouldn't be needing a telephone girl?' asked Amy, and then added hurriedly, 'Just joking, to be sure.'

Bertie looked at her speculatively. She was really a pretty little thing. A bit on the heavy side, but then . . .

'We *are* looking for a girl,' he said slowly. 'It's better to work, Amy, than to sit at

236

home all day living on someone else's money.'

Amy suddenly thought of a day filled with office activity. A day when perhaps this office manager would take her to lunch the way he had once entertained Polly Marsh. She took a deep breath. 'I'd love to work again, Mister Baines.'

'Good!' cried Mr. Baines. 'Why don't you call me Bertie ... when we're not at work of course.'

'Bertie,' said Amy shyly.

She turned and looked around her. Funny how she had never noticed what a pretty place Hampstead was before!

She began to giggle. 'I don't know what Bob will say when he hears my news.'

Mr. Baines frowned. He had already forgotten about Amy's husband. It was such a luxury to relax with someone who looked at you as if you were really important and did not treat you like some type of hilarious joke.

He came to a decision. 'Amy,' he said, 'we have the whole day before we start work tomorrow. Let's go to the zoo!'

'Zoo!' said Amy, clapping her hands. 'You and me?'

'You and me,' repeated Mr. Baines, with

a smile.

He helped her out of her seat and paid the bill.

He tilted his hat rakishly to one side of his head.

He felt like no end of a dog.

★   ★   ★

Bob Friend popped his curly head around the door of his secretary's little room. Miss Jenkins was typing ferociously with myopic concentration.

'I say, Miss Jenkins!'

'Ooh! Mister Friend. You gave me ever such a fright!'

'Would you care to share the old feed bag with me at lunchtime?'

'Ooooh! Mister Friend. Should I *really*?'

''Course you should,' said Bob stoutly. 'Not every day a knight on a white charger comes galumphing along.' He got down on one knee, clasped one hand to his heart, and waved the other in the direction of the enraptured Miss Jenkins. 'I will slay dragons for you. If,' he added, getting to his feet, 'they have any dragons at Spielmann's.'

'Oooh! Mister Friend, you are a one, you

are. Ever such a wag.'

'You'll come for lunch then?'

'Much obliged, I'm sure,' said Miss Jenkins, her eyes like stars, 'and ta, ever so, Mister Friend.'

Bob went off along the corridor, whistling cheerfully.

He, too, felt like no end of a dog.

★    ★    ★

Lady Blenkinsop lay in bed and watched the sun through the lace curtains blazing down on the Mediterranean. It was going to be another perfect day. She reread Bertie Baines's letter for the third time. So he had found a job. And he was prepared to support her if she would return to London and live in some poky hovel in the suburbs.

Why couldn't he have settled down here? It had all been such bliss until he had started to complain that her friends treated him like a gigolo. She had tried to avoid going out into society, but one had to admit that after the first fine, careless rapture had proved that it never could be recaptured, it became rather tedious to be cooped up in a villa in the South of France with the same old dismal face.

She must be philosophical and try to forget about Bertie. But it was a bore that he had been one of those types simply bristling with scruples and morals. Perhaps a gigolo might be a good idea!

She half closed her eyes as a footman came in carrying the wicker breakfast table and began to arrange it on the balcony.

She watched him under her lashes. He had only been in her employment for a week and he really was a splendid figure of a man.

'What is your name?' she asked, and then her face took on the weary, tense look of the well-bred English lady about to plunge into French. '*Comment vous appellez-vous?*'

'Marcel, madame. I spik Engleesh.'

'You do?' Lady Blenkinsop patted the bed. 'Come and sit next to me here, Marcel, and tell me how you learned your English.'

Marcel looked at her speculatively from under his long, curling lashes and then sat down with athletic grace on the edge of the bed.

'Perhaps madame would not like the nature of my education?'

'I am not a snob, Marcel.'

'Oh, no, madame! It is just that my learning of the English was not ...

*convenable.*'

'Ah, Marcel,' she teased. 'Some lady has been teaching you the language *entre les draps.*'

'How did madame guess?' asked the footman, leaning forward languorously.

Lady Blenkinsop looked thoughtfully into his large brown eyes.

'Perhaps, Marcel, it would be a good idea if you locked the door and closed the shutters.'

'Certainly, madame.' He got to his feet and then half turned in the middle of the room. 'Madame will find that I endeavor to give the best service at all times.'

'Splendid!' said Lady Blenkinsop. 'What an intelligent young man you are!'

\*　　\*　　\*

The marquis was thinking about the marchioness as he rode up the long drive toward his home, Granbeigh. Granbeigh was tiny compared to Bevington Chase, but he considered its mellow Tudor brick and rambling lines more pleasing to the eye. His father-in-law had admittedly damned it as a bleeding great pub, but nonetheless he felt it was a perfect setting for his beautiful wife.

He could not help reflecting that Polly's Stone Lane upbringing had turned out to be a marvelous asset when dealing with the tenants. She was genuinely concerned about their welfare, their births, marriages, and deaths. A debutante of his own class, trained in finishing schools and London salons, could hardly have achieved Polly's sympathetic touch.

They had had countless rows, of course, both of them being extremely quick-tempered, but the first year of marriage had gone by rather splendidly.

The Marsh family had returned to Stone Lane after a brief sojourn in the dower house. Unlike Polly, they had found country life far too quiet and had considered the members of the local county uncomfortable and strange animals.

The marquis walked into the drawing room by way of the terrace. There was no sign of his wife. He ambled through the rooms and then finally rang the bell. The butler informed him that his lady had departed very hurriedly after receiving a telephone call from a Mr. Friend.

All the marquis's feelings of contentment and well-being fled. Bob Friend was that

242

good-looking chap who had been made manager of Westerman's. He had always seemed to be a bit too fond of Polly. The marquis began to pace the room. Perhaps Polly—like her parents—secretly found the life of the country dull. Perhaps she found him dull!

By the time another hour had crept past and the birds had begun to chirp sleepily in the ivy, the marquis was convinced that Polly had left him. He remembered all their rows and forgot about their happiness until his marriage seemed a mockery. In his mind's eye he was just shooting Bob Friend dead in the middle of Westerman's when he heard the sound of the carriage wheels on the drive outside.

He crossed to the window, and with a heartfelt feeling of relief, watched his wife descending from the carriage.

Polly trailed miserably into the drawing room. She saw the tall figure of her husband standing by the window and threw herself into his arms. 'Oh, Edward,' she cried. 'I've had such a *beastly* day!'

'Well, it's all your own fault,' said her husband waspishly, 'trailing off to London to consort with office chappies.'

Polly stiffened with anger and wrenched

herself out of his arms. 'If you don't want to listen to me, I shan't tell you,' she said sobbing, and ran from the room.

Cursing himself for a jealous fool, the marquis followed her upstairs and found her lying across her bed crying her eyes out. He sat down on the bed and gathered her gently into his arms. 'I'm sorry,' he whispered against her hair. 'I was jealous.'

Polly dried her eyes and looked at him in amazement. 'Jealous! Of Bob Friend? Oh, Edward! Just wait till I tell you.'

The marquis gathered that Polly had gone straight to Westerman's at Bob Friend's urgent request. Amy had run away with Mr. Baines and was living with him in Highgate. Heatherington's, the firm Mr. Baines was with, had been celebrating their founders' day and had given the staff a day off. Bob planned to go to Highgate and confront them but felt that the presence of the marchioness would do much to bring his guilty wife to her senses.

She had gone to Highgate with Bob and sure enough the guilty pair were at home. Amy had become very thin and painted— and she flounced. She had been wearing a frock with a great many flounces, and it had seemed designed for the excellent purpose

244

of flouncing out of the room when anyone tried to talk to her.

And poor, dear Mr. Baines! What a terrible, *terrible* change. He had been wearing a dreadful double-breasted waistcoat with *lapels*. 'Cad!' murmured the marquis sympathetically. He had been smoking a cheroot right there in the living room, and he had laughed at poor Bob and said that if he didn't know how to appreciate his wife, there were some that did.

There had been nothing to do but leave and she had been heartbroken for poor Bob, who had been silent all the way back to the City.

Westerman's had just been closing and this little office girl with enormous specs had rushed up to the carriage and flung herself into Bob Friend's arms, saying, 'My poor, pwecious Bobsie. Was it terrible?' And Bob had said 'yes,' and he had got down from the carriage and, as he had left with *his arm round the girl's waist*, he had turned and winked at Polly and said, 'Amy ain't the only pebble on the beach.'

'People are so ... so ... *fickle*,' wailed Polly. 'How shall I ever forget this horrible afternoon?'

'Like this,' said the marquis.

'Oh, Edward,' said Polly. 'Before dinner?'

'When else?' said the marquis, unfastening the top button of her dress. 'Consider it part of the hors d'oeuvres.'

'What will the servants think?'

The marquis told the fortunately absent servants to perform an impossible feat with parts of their anatomy and concentrated on the fastenings of his wife's dress.

Polly smiled up at him. 'It was never any use saying "no" to you, my dear marquis.'

'Not the slightest use at all,' he said cheerfully, and that was the last coherent thing the Marquis of Wollerton said for some time.

The publishers hope that this Large Print Book has brought you pleasurable reading. Each title is designed to make the text as easy to see as possible. G. K. Hall Large Print Books are available from your library and your local bookstore. Or you can receive information on upcoming and current Large Print Books by mail and order directly from the publisher. Just send your name and address to:

G. K. Hall & Co.
70 Lincoln Street
Boston, Mass. 02111

or call, toll-free:

1–800–343–2806